PURTOCK

JOHN DUNNE

Anna Livia Press
Dublin

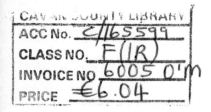
First published in 1992 by
Anna Livia Press Limited
5 Marine Road
Dún Laoghaire
County Dublin

Copyright © John Dunne, 1992

ISBN: 1 871311 20 9 H/B
1 871311 21 7 P/B

Typeset by Michael Ward
Cover and title lettering by Bluett
Printed by Colour Books Limited

Cover features a detail from *Bog Bodies* by Maree Bannon
(courtesy of Laurence O' Neill)

PURTOCK

For John, in memory of Elizabeth

'Love's function is to fabricate unknownness'

e.e. cummings

'Didn't I tell you every word's the truth?'

M.J. Purtock

Everything I am or ever was, all I have pilfered from this begrudging world, my whole life, my fame and what you call my downfall, has come from one thing only. Love. I owe everything to love. Not the sweat between man and woman; not the helpless dependence that parents and their children confuse with love; not the passion for country or idea that men will kill and die for. I am talking of that sensation rushing through your blood; seething in the marrow of your bones; seeping like light from your fingertips; that bewitchment, the one and only love, that makes you want to touch your fellow creatures and, through the simple alchemy of hands, give healing to their lives.

Omnia vincit amor. Master Larkin, how you shape the very words I use.

Go on, shake your heads, snigger at this poor deluded bogman. But I know it's true. Nothing more or less than love.

The finest house, flashiest car, biggest bank account, most learned library, most beautiful ageing wife in this mean provincial town, do not belong to the banker, doctor, big farmer, solicitor or businessman. Because of love, they belong to me. To me, Michael Joseph Purtock, humble offspring of the eternal midland bogs. To me, whose ancestors toiled with flatcher, fork and slane; with barrow, slipe and donkey-cart; who suffered centuries of crooked spines, palms crisscrossed with threads of pain. Season after season, they wrested turf from the squelching earth; stacked and dried it under endless sunblazed skies. Generations of simple countrymen and women, intimate with the ways of skygoat and curlew, the shriek of the otter, the fox's bark at twilight. Countless families of children who ran from Jack O'Lantern flickering in the dark. Modest, faceless people who worked the spongy earth and felt they were in touch

1

with the lurching of the planet.

I can see the eyebrows raised in doubt. The house, car, money, books, wife. How could he achieve all this? This peasant, this yokel, this bogman. You won't have long to wait. I will tell my story to all you strangers, foreigners even, with your cameras, lights, microphones; to you, my unbeloved townsmen, who once stood outside my door in thunderstorm and heatwave; who now, with tales of Miracle Mickey and The Mad Maneen, sell what you swear is my past for pints of slopping porter, fists of ten-pound notes.

I inherited no money, house or land; went to no university; committed no flamboyant crime; grew fat on no rich business deals. You can believe the lies, the rumours flying like turf mould in the wind. You can believe what you like, but listen to me now, and I swear on my mother's grave — like so many I have loved, she was killed by years of sun, wind and rain — that every word's the truth.

Some of you will sneer at the very mention of my beloved bogs. But do you know that in a certain European language the word 'bog' is synonymous with 'god'? There, what do you say to that?

Words. You will learn of my attachment to those sacred scraps of sound you spit at me today. I have always venerated words: their sound, their meaning, their happy or disastrous effects.

How many words have you wasted in a lifetime? Never mind.

I play with words, savour them, marvel at the complexity of their making. Think of *tomb*, for instance. Feel how the tongue glances off the palate, skims the inside of your teeth; how the lips construct the black hole so appropriate to the meaning. I am wasting my breath.

I cry when I remember certain words. I cry for Mary

2

Margaret. Poor never-forgotten Mary Margaret; the tang of creosote on your lips.

All this talk of love and words, I hear you say. Go on then, throw away these words, crumple them in your disbelieving fist, burn them in disgust. But someone will listen. Someone who once was handed to me from his mother's trembling arms, a brittle smile trying hard to mask the pleading in her eyes. I will tell my story to you, or to anyone who listens. To you now, into whose hands these pages filled with truth have somehow found their way.

Listen, my undisbelieving friend, it is not hard to understand.

What? You know nothing of the middle of our island?

Listen. Let every second be a hundred years. Listen and you will hear the almost-silence; feel it throbbing in your veins.

The glaciers have retreated towards the Pole. The Central Plain is pocked with lakes of melted ice. Listen close and you will hear the dying fall of reed and sedge; their slow decay to peat on the bottom of the lake. Look how the layer accumulates until it breaks the surface; how it is invaded by tiny claws of sphagnum whose sorcery with ions will bring acid to the ground.

Imagine vast climatic change; the life and death of trees. All assisting at the birth of my beloved bogs.

But enough of this. Forget such hazy reconstruction. Leap forward four or five millennia and picture this:

The screams have all subsided, the helpless cries are vanished into air. The frightened midland night settles down again. The hare resumes his trodden path; the whiskers of the otter no longer twitch with fear. The timid grouse hides itself; the water-beetle fears no more the tremor in his murky pool. Bullrushes cease their agitated whispers; wisps of bog

3

cotton fall safely to the ground. Dogs locked in outhouses, roped to farmyard trees, leave one ear open and dream of fleshy bones.

Around the cottage, elder trees stand erect again, their branches darker etchings on the blackness of the sky. Inside, kneeling against the bed, a man has collapsed into sleep, his cheek resting on a mess of mangled newspaper and reddened threadbare sheets. He has scrubbed his hands, but blood still darkens underneath the nails. Around the room, buckets of water go slowly cold. A liverish blob bubbles on the hearth.

Inches from the man's head, a woman also sleeps, her face streaked with matted hair and sweat. But look! She is lifting a pale arm and, never once opening her eyes, she moves a palm across her voided belly. Groaning softly, her sleeping hand creeps along the bedclothes and — look! look! — it has found me: Michael Joseph Purtock; only minutes old, my blue lips puckered round the fullness of her breast.

Think long on this, my undisbelieving friend, for this is how it all began. Fill your eyes with the pathetic scene before you; your nostrils with the stench of burning afterbirth. See how the moon hangs astounded in the window.

This is the genesis of Michael Joseph Purtock: clodhopper, rustic, bogman. Renowned Abecedarian, Mad Maneen, Miracle Mickey, Alchemist of Love. Inventor of The Rule of Love. Mortal victim of this accursed town.

How do I know so much of my beginning?

From my parents, especially during the endless years I spent within reach of their hands, or, if their vigilance lapsed, sound of their voices. From hearsay. From my own imagination.

Why did I spend so long at home? You will learn that presently, but first I want to show you where I was born. No child ever knew its own home so well.

You have seen postcards in the city: gleaming white-washed walls, glossy red half-door, four windows, bright yellow thatch. An old couple stands between pots of geraniums; her fingers knotted on a floral apron; his shirt merging with the walls. Stretched in the sunlight, a piebald collie grins at the photographer.

Soak your emigrant's dream in bogwater, dry it near a turf fire, and there you have a picture of our cottage.

It was built by some forgotten ancestor of my father's. No-one knows exactly when, but I recall Master Larkin telling us that you could date a cottage by its windows. Until two hundred years ago, a tax — popularly known as the Typhus Tax — was levied on the size and number of your windows. Peasants had to stint on air and daylight and, so, many died from typhus. Thinking of this now, I am none the wiser about the date, but, then, every word of his affected me like love.

Come with me through the half-door. Sidle past my father's inquisitive ghost, sniff the pipesmoke coiling through the air. Listen carefully and you will hear my mother warning him of fire. Can you hear the derision in his reply? 'Whisht woman, haven't we the leek above on the roof!'

Everyone grew a clump of house-leek in the thatch. It was believed to ward off fire.

Like all the others, our cottage was one room in width for, according to the old ones, bad cess to anyone who presumed to make it wider.

5

You are standing on the flagstone floor. One of my earliest memories is squirming naked in my mother's arms, while she searched me for pismires, who attacked us from the scraws we used to insulate the roof.

Before you are a deal table and three windsor chairs. On the smokegrey wall is stretched an otterskin to protect us from fire. Was any house ever so immune to flames?

For years, I believed my father's story of how, for three days, he fought The Master Otter before finally killing him with a slane, and I was forever asking to touch the scapular of skin which, he said, kept him safe from death by steel or bullet.

To one side hangs my mother's favourite wedding present: a mahogany pendulum clock with the stylised inscription — *Each one hurts. The last one kills.*

To your left, a Welsh dresser stands against a wattle-and-daub partition. Behind this is the bedroom where I uttered my first scream.

On your right is the fireplace with its crane, hakes and ash-hole. And here is the form where Mary Margaret and I huddled together to make up words, or surpass each other with the animals we saw dancing in the flames.

No, of course, our inventions had no meaning, but today, as I caress them in my mouth — *adimba, bdimba, cdimba* — they are more potent than any photograph.

Does the turfsmoke sting your eyes? All through my early years, I never saw that fire go out. Sometimes I still wake at night and my mother kneels before me, pouring ashes on the embers for the morning.

Behind the massive chimney is the parlour, or what everyone called 'the room' — a musty lair of stuffed birds and animals, withered flowers, my mother's paltry heirlooms. All presided over by a daguerreotype of some mutton-chopped relation, his proprietary hand on the seated woman's shoulder; both of them staring more intently than the work of any taxidermist.

I can't remember 'the room' ever used at all until, the evening of my first day at school, I came home to find it had suddenly become my bedroom. I don't know what became of the animals but, often, unable to sleep because of Mary Margaret, I used to wish our disembodied faces through the dark until they settled on the couple in the picture.

Poor Mary Margaret. One of four people who ever loved me and was more than loved in return. How many of us are so fortunate on our journey through this hateful vale of tears?

There is an assortment of oil lamps and, positioned in each room, the aromatic candles my mother made from bog myrtle. A heather broom leans in one corner and, arranged neatly on a shelf, what my father called his 'treasure' — a skull, a cracked wooden bowl, strings of amber beads, a torn black pampootie, arrowheads of iron, flint and bronze.

Eelskins hang drying from the rafters, and, on the wall beside the fireplace, my father's eel-spear with its three serrated blades.

What? You want to hear more about myself? Your silver tongue flatters me.

It is the day before Easter and I am thirteen hours old. A neighbour woman has been to see my mother and left a bottle of holy water propped against the pillow.

Picture this:

My father takes three sips, blesses himself, and offers the

bottle to my mother. Raising herself on one elbow, she drinks and traces a vague cross on her forehead.

Now he fills a spoon and solemnly approaches me. I can imagine this precisely. As the cold edge touches my lips, I start to cry and the water dribbles down my chin. He looks at my mother, but her eyes have closed again. He fills the spoon a second time but it is no use; my face is blue with screaming. My mother turns away and, while he tries to get the water back into the bottle, hides me in her arms.

All that afternoon, while the village preens itself to welcome back the risen Christ, my parents lie beside me. Whenever my screams subside, my father aims his told-you-so smile at my mother's sunken eyes. When suddenly I start again, he storms into the kitchen and attacks the flagstones with a broom. Twice someone knocks on the door, then taps the window-pane. Each time, they are driven away by my father's growl: 'The babby's alright. It's just a bit of wind!'

All that night, while eggs are boiled in washing blue, while children dream of who will eat the most, my mouth is a crimson well of noise.

It is morning now. My mother whimpers as her hand slides away from me and becomes a fist pounding on the pillow. My father fidgets with his belt. Then he rubs his eyes, opens his mouth, but turns without speaking to the Jesus his grandfather carved from a sod of turf. He whispers something and scurries from the room.

I lacerate his prayers as he pulls the donkey from the stable. Any other year at this time, my parents would be returning from the vigil on Easter Hill, their voices filled with wonder at the dancing of the sun. But look at my father now: one minute beseeching Jesus to stop my screams; the next, swearing at the donkey to stand while he fills the cart with straw.

Look how he plunges through the doorway and emerges with wads of clothes; goes inside again and, this time, appears with my mother shrieking in his arms. Soothing her frantic hands, he wraps the clothes around her and, for an instant, it seems that she and I are vying to bawl the loudest. My father is gone a third time, but look! Here he comes striding through the yard with me, in swaddling clothes, clamped against his chest. I melt into my mother's arms as he returns to lock the door. He shouts at the donkey and my mother — poor Madonna of the bogs — starts to howl again.

It is fifteen miles to town and, all along the road, stragglers from The Hill cross themselves as we gallop past their eyes. Women roar at children who drop their coloured eggs, curtains part, birds scatter, dogs chase the wheels as my father lashes the donkey with a stick. I am squealing like a *banbh* in the straw.

By the time we reach the first houses, the donkey's back is bleeding. When it slows into a ragged trot, my father throws away the stick and falls onto the seat, his face nodding in his hands.

A fanfare of tears announces our arrival. Past the crumbling factory, where Hodgson's mechanised dream was a century too soon, trundles our flight from the boglands into Egypt. I see you laugh at my allusion, baulk at such unmitigated bathos, but it springs from yet another part of me haunted by the shade of Master Larkin. Do you want the truth or not?

As we pass beneath the bridge, a train makes the donkey rear in fright and my father topples backwards from his seat. He glances at my mother, swears at the sky, then runs to calm the braying teeth.

From a garden swaying with daffodils, a woman asks if there has been an accident; in reply, my father pummels the donkey with his fists.

A gang of children appears from nowhere and follows us into The Square. Past the blinded windows of the lawyer, whose Latin name will be invoked against me forty years into the future. Around the statue of the Virgin and the horse trough. Past the cinema, where no desperate heroine would ever screech like my mother and I that Easter morning.

My father has never been to a doctor in his life. At the church railing, he asks someone for directions and a young girl peers into the cart. Can you see the picture? A little girl in her Easter bonnet; a cartful of noise with its cortege of giddy urchins. A town given something to laugh about for years; the first sign that The Mad Maneen has come to brighten up their lives. And how they relished my arrival and locked it in their memory. Look, today, how my screams are sold to foreigners.

The girl halts at a Georgian door and stands gaping as my father scatters the children with imaginary stones. He pats my mother's hair, climbs the steps to bang the knocker, then leans on the handrail like someone going to vomit. The girl points to something in the window and he hammers the door again. A woman's head appears and stammers that 'Himself's gone out for his dinner'. As my father jabs the air, the window slams, and the children shout the name of the hotel. The donkey's head is jerked around and my mother's arm dangles like a famine victim's from the cart.

As we near the churchyard a second time, she has fallen silent, but I'm still bawling loud enough to frighten every corpse. Outside the gates, a tinker woman with an apache's head slaps a child, then calmly puffs an inch of cigarette. Is this the same woman who will find the bugleweed for Mary Margaret and, years later, stand before me herself with a baby dying in her arms?

Is it? Could be it? What if? Maybe? What if I was never born? Had never found the primer? Never seen the kitten? Had never known Mary Margaret? If Master Larkin had never crossed the mountain? If the bog had never given her to me? What if? What if? You might as well try to heal the dead.

My father kisses the drooping hand, tucks it beneath the clothes, then leads us up the avenue and through a maze of cars. He pulls me from my mother's grasp, pats the donkey's head, and strides towards the lobby.

Within minutes he is out again, his anger flying like daggers at the doorway. My mother suddenly hauls herself up, clutches at her nightdress, and shrieks 'Where are you taking my baby?' He pushes her back on the straw, drops me on her chest, and tries to drag the donkey through the flowerbeds. It just nibbles at the perfect lawn. Dancing with rage, he tugs its ears and batters the diamond on its forehead.

Cursing every doctor in the country, he scatters clumps of snowdrops with his boot. He attacks the donkey, first with handfuls of clay, then with a young tree. Again and again, he lashes it across the eyes until it stumbles backwards through the flowers. Back and forth we plough until someone shouts from the doorway, and my father pulls us towards the road.

Passing through the gates, he spatters the sign with spit and warns my mother never to stay at that hotel.

Of course this all happened. Would I lie to you? The hotel is still there; go and check for yourself.

Now he is pounding on the presbytery door.

When the housekeeper appears, he roars that his son is going to die and storms past her into the hall. A door opens and the parish priest looks from the woman to the madman

11

with the baby in his arms.

Who knows how that cleric was persuaded — how many masses, First Fridays, loads of turf? — but before my mother knows I'm gone, I am back in her arms again, a strong and perfect Christian with my grandfather's name.

As the donkey shambles off, my father keeps muttering that the child will be alright, the man above will save him.

Is it any wonder I became The Alchemist of Love? Born on Good Friday, baptised on Easter Sunday?

The odyssey of tears is over, but still my shrieks resound against the sky.

My father is standing in the yard, the sun and moon behind him, his arms clasped around the donkey's neck. For a long time he stands like that, then suddenly, as if realising he's being watched, he straightens up and carries me inside.

When my mother and I are back in bed, he pokes life into the fire and, pacing back and forth, waits for the eggs he should have had this morning.

Look at him now, his face a furious mess of tears and yellow slobber. Look how he sends the shells flying, then stops his ears with trembling, sticky hands. Look how his eyes swivel from the table, to the bedroom, to my mother's clock. He stares for ages at the inscription, then pounds the table with his forehead. Like a lunatic, he bangs and bangs until his poor head can take no more and he becomes oblivious to my unearthly wailing.

I was telling you about the cottage.

On one side of the patch of weeds and trodden earth we called the yard, there was the stable, and a shed I used to go to when I wanted to escape my parents' eyes.

I remember the first time. I was three, maybe four, but I eventually succeeded in lifting the bolt and, too frightened to enter, stood gaping as the sun revealed a dazzling nightmare of spikes, chains and blades.

When I was older, I dragged the door behind me, and shivered in the spears of light from knotholes and where blackbirds had pulled scraws from the roof. On the grey walls hung hatchets, coils of rope, trying-irons, a scythe, an armoury of slanes. I inhaled the dead smell and heard the moan of slaughtered animals, the dungeon screams I marvelled at in Master Larkin's history class.

There was also a mildewed pair of pattens, a barrow, wicker baskets, and a slipe on which I closed my eyes and became Saint Nicholas sailing above the bogs to surprise the village children.

In late summer, my father built a rick against the eastern gable. This was my first calendar, and the days to spring were measured by the removal of each sod. The space was always cleared just in time for the next harvest, and my father's calculations made me love him all the more. I can still see myself, standing on the bare rectangle, wondering how such weight had floated up the chimney.

A screen of elders stood between the bog lane and the yard. Their heavy scent, my mother told me, kept butterflies from her cabbage, and the fermented berries could ease the most distressful cough.

Leave the yard through the rickety wooden gate, turn right and your thoughts fill with town; right again, and you are heading towards the bog. But go left at the gate and you will meet the first of our neighbours' cottages. This belongs to my father's brother Joseph and, as you will see, I grew to know it as intimately as my own.

Mary Margaret lived in the next house — identical to ours, bar the extra room which defied all superstition to accommodate her bulging family. Fecundity. Uberty. Philoprogeneity. Look them up yourself. No doubt you've been told about the banker's wife who came at the dead of night and whinged until I let her in? How I demanded a written guarantee of sex when her body returned to normal. Did you ever hear the likes? Lies, all lies! The Rule of Love never needed any carnal satisfaction.

We called it a village, but Tonelemona was more a row of cottages with its arse to the bog. In the year I was born, the 'statistics' were as follows:

> Cottages: 15
> Men (over eighteen): 22
> Women (over eighteen): 24
> Boys: 20
> Girls: 27
> Donkeys: 24
> Horses: 10
> Cows: 11

There were also various outhouses, a school, a ruined chapel, a graveyard, and a forge. Any number of fowl and domestic animals, a pet fox, and The Widow Tynan's shop.

Here's a story for you:

Jimmy Tynan is barely settled in the ground, and Billy-the-Box has hardly hung up his tools, when Mary rips the money from the mattress and sends for him again. He is put hammering in 'the room' while she disappears on Jimmy's ass and cart. Next morning, a dray arrives in the yard and Mary stands cackling while the driver stocks the village's first shop. That evening, GENERAL STORE, in dripping red letters, appears above the door.

This happened years before my time, but, later on, I knew The Widow as a dumpy little woman with a passion for Zane Grey. Throughout my childhood, she was 'never short a sugarstick for the poor maneen'. Only once did I ever see her angry: the morning she tore the silver paper from my nervous copper, and swore a cuckoo's child would never come to any good.

That single room sold everything and anything from galvanized buckets to tinned meat and Woodbines; clay and liquorice pipes, axel grease and Mrs Cullen's Powder. In summertime, a shelf of cranberry jam, turf ornaments, sprigs of rosemary and ling lay in wait for the occasional tourist who might wander from the town.

It wasn't until I was six or seven that I realised just how diverse her business was. We were gathering sticks for Saint John's bonfire when, as we passed the shop, raucous singing split the air. I strained to catch my mother's disgust, and poteen dribbled its way into my teeming pool of words.

Neighbours arriving to hansel me were stopped by a wall of noise. Fingering the silver in their pockets, they murmured a quick prayer and turned away again. Their gossip became the bedrock of my legend.

The more my mother begged that I be brought back to the doctor, the more my father refused. So, despite the novenas to Saint Blaise, the relics stitched inside my clothes, the statues paraded round and round my bed; despite all my mother's ointments and decoctions, silence never came near the cottage until the first day of April. No doubt you'll see significance in the date. Don't.

Look. My father is on his knees emptying the ash-hole when a scream explodes from the bedroom.

'He's asleep. He's fast asleep. My baby's fast asleep!'

He drops the shovel, runs inside and stands as if moidered, eyes and mouth wide open, palms pressed to his astounded ears.

How was the family affected by its *via dolorosa*?

For my father, it confirmed his hatred of the Hippocratic trade. For my mother, it was a sign that her child was touched by God, or something worse. And myself? Perhaps it sowed the seeds of my conviction that the bogman can expect nothing from the town. All I know for certain is it caused the hoarseness in my voice that annoys me to this day.

At three weeks old, while the world's most favoured nurslings were yet to even babble, I, poor child of the brown bogs, could enunciate the five vowels. Spheres of perfect sound floating through the smoky air to infinity beyond. And that's not all. Shortly after, I had mastered the art of lallation, a feat my mewling contemporaries would struggle with for another six or seven months. Of course I'm serious. Didn't I tell you every word's the truth?

Were my parents surprised? Certainly not. Why should they be? Visitors may have remarked on the clarity and range of my loquacity, but, after all, was I not the firstborn son, the apple of my mother's eye, who had slipped from her womb without the benefit of medicine or nurse; without the intervention of anyone but my father? In his terror and delight, he certainly never thought of measuring this mite of squirming flesh. He would have found that I was a fraction more than thirteen inches.

It is early May and, like medieval pilgrims, my barefoot village converges on the bog. Shoulders bristling with flatchers, slanes, and spades, they chatter and look occasionally at the sky. Some push barrows; others lead donkeys and swear when the slipe glances off a rock. A few old men carry trying-irons and dream of unearthing another boat like the one The Zulu Galvin sold to the museum. Women bring blackened kettles, cakes of bread, milk in bottles stopped with rags. My mother is carrying me.

What?

His grandfather joined the British Army and was killed somewhere in the Transvaal.

The drainage channels have been dug and now, working

backwards in a line, they strip the top spongy layer. This 'fum' makes bad firing but will be welcomed by the poor.

What?

Of course there were. Do you think the bog is some sort of Utopia, a middle-class Arcadia?

Ambo florentes aetatibus, Arcades ambo. Mary Margaret and I. What? Nothing. You wouldn't understand.

Now and then someone calls, and children run to a hare's nest, or timidly approach a tussock where the stonechat's fear is like pebbles rattling in a bag. My mother is with the old women searching for tormentil, whose roots will make red dye or, boiled in milk, banish diarrhoea. Smiling to herself because she knows how he'll react, she tears a sprig of rosemary to stitch inside my father's cap. She says it wards off headache.

Apart from the scrapers, no-one wears shoes. Why? Because the bog cures every known infection of the foot, that's why. I remember my father telling me how, during the war, the village gathered tons of sphagnum to make dressings for the wounded.

There is no place healthier than my beloved bogs. Unlike your foreign moors and fens, which sometimes breathe malaria, you will find no mephitic vapours here. And did you know that town gas was once purified by crushed iron found right behind our cottage? Of course you didn't. And still you townies scoff at the bogman. How many of you drowse by turf fires in the winter? How many of your wives ooh and aah at Joe Lalor's carvings, then snigger at 'how quaint these people are'? Do you know Joe Lalor's work? 'A naive master from the Midlands', the gallery called him. We called him 'Joe the Head'. No? Remind me again. I want to tell you about my father now.

Above the Brueghel landscape, a skylark is a fluttering

speck of song; along its edges the snipe's 'chipper chipper' lures children to the birch trees. When the sun is at its highest, a woman calls across the moneen and, for twenty minutes, the men relax; eating, smoking, bantering about each other's work.

As if on signal, they rise together and, following the custom of centuries, divide into four groups — cutters, catchers, wheelers and spreaders. It is now my father comes into his own. The slane is a special type of spade with a wing set at right angles to the blade. This allows the cutter to take out a complete sod each time. It is the quintessential emblem of our village. Someday I'll design a Purtock coat-of-arms. I can see it already. Dexter flank, tenney, a slane proper. Sinister flank, azure, a curlew passant. Middle base, vert, a donkey rampant.

Of course I know what it means. What do you think I had in the library? Turf? Or maybe just a field gules, The Rule of Love statant?

My father was the most celebrated *sleadóir* in the Midlands. 'Straightface Purtock' they called him. No, nothing like that. He could keep a perfectly straight face on every bank he cut and, all my life, I heard him sneer at those he called 'clodcutters'. And why shouldn't he? No-one should ever have to suffer fools. As the crackling of thorns under a pot, so is the laughter of a fool.

Come closer and watch him now. One stroke and the blade penetrates the ground; another, and the squelching sod is free; a third lifts; a fourth and the sod is on its way towards the catcher. My father could keep three men going for a day. One. Two. Three. Four. A tetrad perfect as the sounds that made my mother cry with love that evening in 'the room'.

What?

19

Nothing.

The catchers stack the sods on barrows which the wheelers then push to the *scair*, a drying-place nearby, though sometimes a slipe is used on mucky ground. The upper, lighter sods — which we burned in summertime — were always taken furthest away. The black bottom turf was spread nearest to the bank.

But I can see you have had enough. Even you, my undisbelieving friend.

Why do people hate the bogs? Why will they scrimp and save to visit windy seaside towns; cities smothered in filth; mountains transformed by visions into money-traps for the curious, the lonely and the dying?

But how many will 'broaden their minds' by entering the watery kingdom of the boglands? If it wasn't for me, do you think there would be a sinner here today? Michael Joseph Purtock, tourist attraction, economic saviour of the Midlands. You think I'm arrogant? Should I lie down and whinge because of what they're doing to me? I was born to laugh at hurricanes.

Why do people travel? I will tell you why. It makes them feel important. The more they see, the more their dominance is confirmed: 'Look at us, we bested mountains, tamed the sun, shaped the air to accommodate our dreams.'

And every work of art becomes a mere reminder of their power. This picture, book, symphony, cathedral . . . . 'One of ours did that!' And you accuse me of arrogance.

But their vanity — which everywhere else they wear like a crown — is threatened by the bog, intimidated by its apathetic vastness. Hearts beat fast, a shiver crawls along the spine, and something keeps telling them how helplessly alone, how utterly insignificant they are in this *terra incognita* of endless air and water.

Did you know that the bog is ninety-five per cent water? Less solid matter than milk!

And how do they disguise their fear? They call it boredom: 'But it's so featureless. How could anyone exist here?'

I will tell you about existence. The quaking ground, the invisible gurgling of streams, the smallest sprig of heather, the most transparent insect, have all been here for millennia without you, and will continue for ages more to come. And what have you? Seventy? Eighty? Ninety? A hundred at the outside. Mayflies. Poor deluded mayflies the lot of you.

The Rule of Love is patient and kind. The doctor's married daughter. Anorgasmia. Please don't tell Daddy. Yes Yes. Don't tell anyone. Yes Yes Yes . . . . It envieth not, dealeth not perversely, is not puffed up. The chambermaid from the hotel. The smell of sweat and fish. Tears of blood on the donkey's face. It is not ambitious, seeketh not its own, is not provoked to anger. The banker's wife groping in the bedclothes for her cheque-book. It thinketh not evil, rejoiceth not in iniquity, but rejoiceth with the truth. The blonde tourist. *Ja mein Liebling, Ja, Ja.* It beareth all things, believeth all things. The tang of creosote. Mary Margaret gaping at the stars, her nightdress spread around her. It hopeth all things, endureth all things. A dog's head grinning from the black pool. The Rule of Love never faileth. The earth trembles, a hand appears from the bog. The room evaporates in creosote. The Rule of Love is patient and kind . . . .

Tell me this. After love, what is the second most important thing in life? Sex? Health? Power? Money? Happiness? Death? None of these. It is sleep. Sleep that knits up the ravell'd sleave of care. I've hardly slept a wink in ages. How can I, with their lights poking my eyes every few minutes? I am living an insomniac's nightmare. Like Macbeth, they have murdered sleep. Why? Because they fear my dreams, that's why. Because they know I dream the truth.

And the questions they keep asking:

Did you love your mother?

Did you love your father?

Why were you an only child?

Did anything ever happen in your childhood?

Jesus, do they not know who they're talking to? I am Michael Joseph Purtock, Dreamer of Truth, the one and only Alchemist of Love.

While they were still fingering dirty pictures, I had studied books they have only heard about. *The Interpretation of Dreams, Psychopathia Sexualis, Claustrophobia in the Midlands*: I have read them all. Read them all and laughed.

You asked about the chapel. Although it happened years before I was born, I have heard the story so often I know it by heart.

Everyone loved Paddy Lambe. At first it was pity. People came to see Mrs Lambe's new baby and, as if by sharing its signs, they might lessen his affliction, they took home with them a different form of pity. Pity for the roundness of his face; for the folds of skin around each slanting eye; for the brain that made him different. Is is any wonder they called him 'The Lamb of God'?

As he grew up, this compassion turned to love; the sort of love we keep for sick neighbours and animals; the sort of love that costs nothing, yet makes us proud for giving it. Cynical? What is cynicism? A ruthless insistence on the truth, a refusal to be moved by every cheap emotion, that's what. Does it make you feel good to help a blind man across the street; sit for hours with your bedridden neighbour? Well, does it? And what do you feel when you have to make excuses for your child's stupidity, or nurse your senile mother? Well, tell me, what do you feel? Pure unselfish love?

And another thing. Suppose there has been a tragedy, or any kind of accident. Do you not, even for an instant, enjoy that little thrill, the merest tic of superiority, when you tell your friends how well you know the victim? Liar.

Don't talk to me of love. All my life I have given it away like smiles, and look at me today.

The Lamb of God was always up to something. He could barely walk when he knocked over a kettle and scalded Mrs Galvin's cat. A few years later, he managed to hack the tail off his father's donkey, and scattered The Widow Tynan's shelves when she refused to buy the 'hairy snake' he swore he had captured in a bog-hole.

From the day he was born, the Health Board tried to take him, but, with each new escapade, the village grew to love him more. Every house was his own, and he spent his days straying like a dog from door to door. My father often told me how he would appear in the yard with an armful of clothes from someone's line, and cheerfully announce that he was coming for his holidays.

Even after the episode with the hens, my grandparents still loved him as their own. They arrived home one evening from the bog to find half their precious Leghorns frantic in the yard, the rest cowering in the elders like embryonic creatures aghast at their untimely birth. And there was The Lamb of God, clutching gusts of feathers like a child chasing snow. The poor fool was so happy that all my grandfather could do was swallow his rage and crush him to his chest. Everyone loved The Lamb of God.

But here is the story of the chapel:

It is the coldest Christmas in living memory; so cold that, on their way to midnight mass, the villagers never even think about the cock. It was an old belief that the cock crowed with delight on Christmas Eve, and good luck was sure to follow whoever heard it first.

It is so cold inside the chapel that Father Moran's breath rises like incense from the altar. He is washing his fingers when, calm as you like, The Lamb of God strolls up the centre aisle, the candle held before him like a flower. Women smile; the men slip him roguish winks as he genuflects before the sanctuary and turns towards the crib.

Love turns to bemusement; freezes in a mask of horror as it dawns on them what he's trying to do.

The cruets clatter to the ground and Father Moran scurries down the steps. He grabs a paten from the altar-rail and, as if surrounded by wasps, attacks the cloud of smoke. The Lamb of God screams 'I'm keeping Baby Jesus warm', and lunges forward, straight into the paten's silver edge. The villagers sit like statues as a collar of blood erupts on his throat.

He dances for a moment, then collapses on the straw.

Baby Jesus burns like a sacrificial victim. The paint on Mary's face blisters and bursts, leaving the black holes of some medieval plague.

Someone drags The Lamb of God from the crib and Father Moran bends over him, feverishly whispering in his ear.

The crib is now a roaring furnace. The altar cloths, advent banners, even the flowers, are burning. The sanctuary lamp crashes to the ground, but it is not until my grandfather carries out the body that the villagers scramble down the aisle.

Bent before the tabernacle, Father Moran's face is whiter than his alb. Someone roars that the roof is going to fall and, slowly, as if leading a procession, he turns towards the door.

Feet snap the brittle grass as they flee across the churchyard, mothers screaming for children, men carrying old women on their shoulders. The noise abates to a low prayer as they gather round The Lamb of God. Above their heads, wisps of straw are red scratches on the darkness; the moon is a coin with the head of God the Father.

Two nights later, amid the smell of charred wood and the grief of the entire village, The Lamb of God was buried. Mass was nearly over when Father Moran's voice began to falter: '*Agnus Dei, qui tollis . . . agnus dei . . . agnus dei . . . agnus dei . . . .*'

He never finished, but burst his way through the ring of mourners, the whimpered Latin hanging like apologies in his wake. '*Agnus dei. . . agnus dei . . . agnus dei. . . .*'

Next morning he was gone and, despite years of pleading by the priests in town — even, my father used to sneer, the bishop's threat of mass-excommunication — there would never be another chapel in the village.

At twelve months, not only did I know my own age, but I could sit for hours, calmly producing page after page of immaculate cephalopods — a feat which, in any culture you care to mention, would elicit gasps of admiration for the most precocious two-year-old. Imagine, I could have been an artist too!

In the English language there are seventeen vowels and twenty-seven consonants. By the age of two, I had them all. Every single one. I could impress you with my knowledge of close, plosive, fricative, flapped, but all you need to know is that I was no tongue-tied Philip Pirrip. Observe me as I waddle through the yard, squawking like some exotic bird: 'MICHAELJOSEPHPURTOCK! MICHAELJOSEPHPURTOCK!'

But I am no braggart. James V was king of Scotland before he reached his second year. Grimaldi, king of clowns, was performing at the same age. So, I ask you, what is a prodigy? Someone who is different from the rest, that's all.

Leonardo claimed that every man at three years old is half his eventual height. He may have known how to paint on walls, capture enigmatic smiles, but when it came to paediatrics he should have shut his mouth. It's your average two-year-old who has reached the halfway stage.

What am I trying to prove? Nothing. Nothing at all, but on the morning of my second birthday, my mother took a tape from her sewing box, stood me against the kitchen wall and, to her horror, found all her prayers unanswered.

A what? Don't ever use that word again! What do you think I am? Something in a circus? Some sort of freak tumbling after Snow White? Listen. I am The Alchemist of Love, inventor of The Rule of Love, who, at the age when parents drool over every squeak their little darlings make, could recite the entire vocabulary of the bogs.

You asked about my parents.

My mother was a deeply religious woman immersed in superstition. In her prayers, Jesus, Mary and the Child of Prague jostled with the *pooka*, *dullahán*, and May Day hare. Like all our neighbours, she never went to mass, yet ran to kiss the biretta when the priest appeared from town. I inherited her eyes, perfect skin (I didn't need to shave till I was twenty), her modesty and infinite patience, but I drew the line at seventh sons, falling pictures, and robins in the kitchens. I loved my mother for her hands — can you hear my father's laughter as she washes them in the dew? I loved her for the untimely whiteness of her hair, for the way she never stopped telling me how much she loved me.

My father. Peasant and avatar of the bogs. I loved him for his hands, for the strength of his slane, for his helpless tears whenever I hurt him. I loved him for his hatred of the town; for his cap that never hid the port wine stain; for the donkey's hoof; the thread of blood on his cheek. I loved him for his face when Nan-the-Habit laid him out.

On a warm August night, as the last of the turf was stacked against the gables, Master Fitz was carried to the graveyard. Heralded by weeks of speculation, John Larkin arrived on the last Sunday of the month and, next morning, reopened the school. That evening, eager voices ran to tell his story to the village:

He was tall as trees; he was the same size as Master Fitz.
His wife was dead; she was coming next week.
He had a bicycle; he always rode a donkey.
He was cross; he was easy.
He preferred the girls; he liked the boys best.
He came from the city; he was from a village in the west.

On Tuesday, the priest arrived to welcome him, and the swirl of rumour settled into a few accepted facts. He was a bachelor in his thirties, fond of bicycling, and a native of the county beyond the mountains. He was a pinnacle of pedagogic achievement who, the priest impressed upon his listeners, brought with him the most impeccable references of character.

The Widow Tynan said he looked like a cross between a hedge-school master and a country squire.

I dreamed this the other night:

When my mother leaves the door ajar, I crawl inside and, followed by the eyes of ancestors and birds, investigate every nook and cranny of 'the room'. Now and then, I pause at specks of dirt and try them in my mouth.

On my belly, face squashed white against the cupboard, grunting till the veins corrugate my neck, I stretch and strain until, at last, I have it. A spider scuttles away as I smell the mould and flick at cobwebs with my tongue. I have found *The Children's ABC*, published by The National Education Board in 1877.

Look closely, for there on that damp floor, eyes wide in the brownish light, I am immersed in the radiance of words. My mother stands in the doorway and loves me all the more

for the magic tumbling from my mouth. A is for Arm, B is for Bed, C is for Cart, D is for Donkey . . . .
Of course I knew what they meant. Weren't there pictures? Sometimes I wonder why I tell you anything. Did it really happen? Does it matter?

The Alphabet became the *lares et penates* of my childhood and by the age of three or four I was a legend.

As if dispensing charity, or trying to appease the ogre in a fairytale, the villagers left ragged almanacs and books, yellowed issues of the The Midland Star on the doorstep, then went away to joke about The Mad Maneen.

I devoured The Widow Tynan's Westerns and my grandmother's Bible from Genesis to Revelation. All the nights I fell asleep in a coat of many colours, a six-gun pointed at the looming jawbone of an ass. The nights a white horse thundered from the bog across my dreams of gold and silver, ivory, apes and peacocks. I was a brother to dragons, a companion to owls. Do you know that? Hah! Pearls before swine.

I read the labels on everything in the house, then leaned across the gate, chanting the most obscure ingredients and compounds. I interrogated passersby for details of marriages and births, court cases, auctions in the county ten, twenty, thirty years ago. Imagine visiting the cottage, and there is yours truly, hunched like an old man at the fire, calling out the death notices from the paper. Deeply regretted by. Interment immediately afterwards in adjoining cemetery. American papers please copy. Imagine that. Poor Mary Margaret.

But was I really so extraordinary?

Macaulay was an omniverous reader at three; Mozart and Mahler were composing before they reached five. And what about that little girl who gave birth at the same age?

I warned you before, don't ever think of me as some sort of aberration, a freak of nature, a curiosity found in the bog. I am The Alchemist of Love. No more. No less. Just The Alchemist of Love. Listening to them today, you would think I had horns. Do you know that famous statue of Moses? Well, there you are. Explain that!

The sods have been drying for weeks, and now the workers gather beneath a flawless sky. Driven by the pulse of centuries, their bodies bend and rise to stack the turf in *coirceoga*, cone-shaped heaps which expose new surfaces to the sun and wind.

I am with my mother near the cromlech. She loves sitting here. She says it makes her feel how long our people have been living on the bogs. But she will never step inside the stones, and it is years before I discover why.

Look how her needle flashes in the light; how I scatter verses through the air:

> The time has come, the Walrus said,
> To talk of many things,

Of shoes, and ships, and sealing wax,
Of cabbages and kings.

My mother snaps the thread with her teeth and, leaning
back against a stone, Mrs Dunne smiles at me, then returns
her gaze to the infant in her arms. Mary Margaret is three
weeks old. Watch her fingers clutch at nothing, her lips
squeeze the blueveined breast. Lips that all the magic of my
hands, all the creosote in the world, will not save from
crumbling into clay.

Within weeks of his arrival, the entire village agreed how
wonderful Master Larkin was; how fortunate they were that
he had come among them.

Children, whose hands still trembled at the thought of
Master Fitz, loved the way he stroked their hair; how the
sound of his beloved Latin sailed beyond their spellbound
ears.

No, of course it wasn't an 'official' subject, but no-one
ever left his classroom without some awareness of what we
owed to ancient Rome.

The world was older now than the children had ever
imagined. At mealtimes, the day's work, predictions for the
winter, even Grace, were shouted down by tales of Romulus
and Remus or the knife that finished Caesar. As they day-
dreamed into sleep, donkeys trudged across the bog through
clouds of ice to Italy; their mothers' chickens hissed intrud-
ers from the seven hills.

Nodding in admiration as, one after the other, he pinned
their arms to The Widow Tynan's counter, the men looked

31

forward to his strength when cutting began in spring. They envied the straightness of his spine, his easy confidence with strangers, how quickly he had won the devotion of their children. But, most of all, it was his recitations that charmed the dourest heart.

I see you're grinning at the very notion of a bogman appreciating poetry, but ask anyone who was ever there. And no, it wasn't all 'Nell Flaherty's Drake' or 'A Mother's Love's a Blessing'.

When The Master's desolation stilled that jovial room, even Billy-the-Box, who in his time had coffined tiny children, gazed at his boots and blessed the smoke that stung his eyes:

> You took my East and you took my West,
> You took before and after from me.
> You took the moon and you took the sun,
> And I greatly fear that you took my God.

Poor Mary Margaret; your ravaged lips pleading to the stars.

Whenever he saluted them from his bicycle, women reddened and pictured him without his clothes. When they passed his cottage in the dark, they pointed to the romantic profile reading in the lamplight. But more than anything, they fell in love with his mystery. Why was such a handsome man still single at his age?

My father does not see me watching through a sliver in the curtains. I wait until he comes back in and tell him I have left a book outside. He warns me not to disappear.

Wobbling on a platform of turf, I fish around inside the rainbarrel. The fur feels like wet feathers as I hold it to my cheek. With one eye on the door, I breathe on the white nose and softly close the lips over the minuscule teeth. Over and over again, wishing like the child in the fairytale, I caress the sodden body. Then slowly, as if stretching in its sleep, a paw moves and something tremors through its length. Its mouth opens and closes like a fish.

My hands have triumphed over death. My hands are the resurrection and the life.

I release it into the ditch and tell my father I can't find the book.

I dream about it still. For days it prowls across the bog; struggles through nets of heather, peeps through grass at the kestrel's 'kee kee kee', stabs at tiny tussock moths, until it reaches the cave at Clonmacnoise. There it is welcomed by the King of Cats, and lives its life as sentry against children who, in the hope of making him speak, come with knives to take a piece from its master's ear.

Any fool can dream of falling over edges. I dream the truth.

Uncle Joe is slurping tea from a saucer when I emerge from the bedroom with *Gulliver's Travels* in my hand. He asks when the scholar is going to school, and even I am surprised by how vehemently my father spits 'He's not.' Joe says his John can't wait to start and, as my mother's voice rises, her look tells me to get back to bed. I open my mouth to protest, but my father's glare propels me through the door. A minute later, my mother leaves a lamp on the locker by my bed.

I try to distract myself with stories about The Master

Otter, but it's no use. I crane my neck and words penetrate the wall.

Doctors.

Teachers.

Bastards.

I hear nothing for a while, then 'runt' explodes from Joe. My mother screams at him to get out and leave her house forever. The door slams and the flame flickers in its globe. When the shadows quieten, I listen again. The bucket is scraping on the flagstone as my mother prepares the fire for the morning.

They climb into bed on either side of me and, before kissing me goodnight, his deep voice says 'It's ages since we've seen your Uncle Joe.' She grunts something I'm not supposed to understand and smothers me in her arms.

For the first seven years of my life, I was pampered in my parents' bed. My eyes closed in their arms and awoke in them again. Is it any wonder I remained a cuckoo's child?

Can you sum up your childhood in a word? I can. Hands. No matter what I did; where I tried to go; proud, loving, frightened hands rested on my shoulder, caressed my face, held my wayward fingers. The immanence of hands. Hers softened by the dew, his pocked with cuts and scabs. I was a small wounded creature; the world one warm benevolent hand. That was my childhood.

That's one version. Here's another:

The slightest unfamiliar sound and I am rooted to the ground, unable even to breathe for fear his whip will flick out my eyes. On dark evenings I shiver at the curtains, waiting for his headless horse to gallop past the gate. If ever I dare leave the yard, he is lurking in the bushes, a basin of blood poised above his headless neck. Lying in my parents' warmth, I see my eyes blinded, my face a sticky crimson mask. My mother's *dullahán*: the grim keeper who ensured I never fled the prison of her love.

Both versions are the truth.

My father was gone hunting foxes when The Mitching Man knocked the door. Did you ever try to catch the wily Reynard?

What?

Must I explain everything? Did your mother never read you stories? I suppose there's no point in telling you it comes from the Gothic word *raginohart*, or that the fox itself symbolises the Catholic Church?

What do you mean 'so what?'

Listen, and don't ever forget this: there is no such thing as useless knowledge. Every thought that flits across my brain, every word that passes through my lips is sacred. That's what.

Where was I?

When I was older, my father used to bring me with him and, back and forth across the county, I became the Nimrod of my dreams. He had heard somewhere that there was a bounty for every tongue presented at the barracks.

But that's not what I want to tell you. Listen to this:

It was just before Christmas that I saw my father angry for the second time. I was searching for a wren in the elders when I saw the fox. I poked it with a stick; then, crawling through the ditch, felt the rigor mortis with my boot. I knew straightaway my hands were useless. An inch of frosty tongue protruded from its snarl. I ran to the shed, found a knife, and was hacking at the mouth when I felt my father glaring at my back. In a sudden cloud of breath, he growled for the knife, and was raising his hand to hit me when my mother called from the yard. Muttering, he turned and strode away.

But I've gone ahead of myself again.

I was playing with the abacus my mother made from rosehips when The Mitching Man arrived. I gawked from behind her skirt as she told him why I wasn't going to school. He listened politely, then recited the details of such and such an Act. When he had finished, she asked would the government cure her child, and quietly told him never to darken her door again.

That evening, Master Larkin came to the cottage. My father was calling us to come and see the foxes, when he appeared at the gate in a tweed suit and shining oxblood boots. He saluted my mother, tousled my hair, and introduced himself to my father who, in reply, barked at me to go inside.

Through the window, I watched my parents stand close together, not even nodding as the Master's mouth moved up and down.

When he was gone, I ran into the yard and sniffed his polish in the air.

Over the next few weeks, The Mitching Man and Master Larkin came again; followed by the priest who had baptised me, and a policeman from the town. No-one ever said a word to me, but I was seven before my parents let me go to school.

My father's lips moving as he struggles with my books.

The smell of soap and warm towels; the slippery feel of my own skin; the soft grey touch of galvanize; my mother humming as she kneels beside the bath.

My father's curses on the town.

My mother's sewing-box. Her tears.

The average height of a five-year-old boy is forty-five inches. On my fifth birthday, my mother stood me against the wall again. I was thirty inches.

My father clears his throat, glances at my mother, and asks him if all the crying could have broken something in my brain; a nerve, a tube or something that makes people grow.

The old man's breath is like something dead and, as he measures me with his hands, I try to see different countries in the tea-stains on his shirt.

I am tired standing. For ages we have traipsed across the bog, their voices hurting me like slaps across the face.

'Why won't you bring him?'

'Don't ever mention those bastards again!'

'Stubborn as usual!'

'What good will Mooney do?'

'Didn't he cure Billy Keegan!'

The more they shout, the tighter my mother squeezes my hand. I try to stop them by pointing to a line of curlews, or the metallic glint of a damselfly. But I am talking to the air. When his curses make her hand hurt mine, I lie about the millions of eels I see wriggling from a bog-hole. But he doesn't even offer me a glance.

From my father's derision, I expected some sort of witch's cave with eyes blazing from the gloom. But it is only a cottage much like our own. Smaller and dirtier, but still an ordinary bogland dwelling, even if it stands alone in acres of wind and sky. And despite my fear, I am disappointed.

I stiffen when the old man tells me to undress. My father coughs again, but my mother steps forward, warns me to do what Mr Mooney says, and I am suddenly naked on the clay floor. There is no sound but my breathing as he holds a forked hazel switch before my face. He says something from the corner of his mouth, but all I can make out is Queen Victoria and Saint Francis of Assisi. As if I'm something that might pounce, his eyes never leave mine. Mumbling words even I have never heard, he begins to shuffle in a circle, the hazel trembling like a crucifix in the hands of an exorcising priest.

I can feel my eyes burning and, for the first time in my life, I know for certain I am not like other children. There is something wrong with me. Something terrible that makes them want to embarrass me like this. The fetid breath scalds the back of my neck and I know I am going to wet myself. As if it was my own blood, I stare at the dark continent forming on the clay.

On the way home, no-one says a word. See how my father strides ahead, his face blanker than the sky. Look at my mother, her headscarf hiding the tears I know are making her face ugly. Look at me, The Mad Maneen, jerked along by her rigid hand, searching my beloved bog for an answer to my question. What have I done to anger those who love me?

I saw Mooney in the crowd today. Spitting at a camera how he knew for a fact that I had consorted with the Devil.

The sods are bone-dry now, and the villagers, with slipes, carts and donkey creels — even the oldest women with kishes slung across their shoulders — are bringing them from the bog.

Without fear of contradiction, I can tell you that Tonelemona is the finest bog in the country. Unlike the southern turf you can bend across your knee, or that grey mush from the west — did you ever soak a loaf of bread and try to lift it with a fork? — ours is dark, almost black, and dries as hard as rock.

You don't believe me? Try it yourself and see. Full refund if not delighted.

Whatever the village doesn't need is sold at weekends in the town, but, ever since the Easter of my birth, my father cursed my mother's fears of how she would manage through the winter, and steadfastly refused to 'have any truck with them bastards and their highfalutin ways'.

My mother and Mrs Dunne are in their usual spot by the cromlech. Lolling at their feet, Mary Margaret and I tear the starry petals from clumps of asphodel. The women smile as our voices rise in a shrill, malicious chant:

> One for the donkey, two for the cow,
> Three for the horse, you'll do no damage now.

This small yellow plant — it turns a lovely orange in autumn — was feared and hated by the village because animals grazing on it developed brittle bones. I was with Uncle Joe the evening his donkey tripped on a tussock. I can still hear the foreleg snapping like a stick. It screamed and hobbled a few yards before collapsing on its side. Joe warned me not to move and ran back to the village.

It took me ages to calm the frantic hooves. I was whispering in the donkey's ear when Joe returned with the shotgun and told me to go home quick, my mother wanted me straightaway. When I hesitated, he said he would count to three . . . . I knew my parents would never let the donkey die, so I raced until my lungs burned my chest.

I found my mother in the yard, shouting after my father as he disappeared inside the shed: 'He's the same as all the Purtocks. Why didn't he send for Bartle Mooney?' Just as my breath stopped hammering, and words tried to gather in my throat, her red face turned and ordered me into the house.

I don't know about 'all the Purtocks', but, because I could never watch the smallest creature suffer, I was certainly like Uncle Joe. My cousin John used to taunt me when I would cry over the skylark's broken eggs, or run away when he'd stick a straw in a frog and blow until it was as bloated as his cheeks.

Don't for one minute believe all that tourist guff about the quaintness, the 'simple bucolic pleasures of the boglands'. When it came to cruelty, the children of Tonelemona were as casual as children anywhere. Do you know the biggest myth of all in this accursed two-faced world? The innocence of childhood. There is no such thing. Never was and never will be. I have seen families torn apart by the wickedness of children. Little girls of ten, eleven, twelve, more impudent than any whore. Boys who would knife you for the pennies in your pocket. And who can blame them? What example are they shown? Look at me. A lifetime devoted to love, and what have I been given in return?

But that's not what I wanted to tell you. Why am I so easily distracted? Could it be the food? After everything else, I wouldn't put it past them. Maybe they're slipping something into it? Something to confuse me and keep me from the truth? Grey stew with a *bouquet garni* of sodium pentothal *à la* the Minister of Health? Paranoid? You're naive. They have every sort of poison here. I'm telling you, I've seen it. It's like the palace of the Borgias. That's what I'll call them; Cesare and Lucrezia. The one that tries so hard to make me like him. Please Mister Purtock this. Sorry Mister Purtock that. The one with the bonsai sprouting from her cheek. I know what I'll do. Something that will really drive them mad. I'll refuse to eat until they appoint a taster. How will they explain it when, like King John's monk, the poor fool's bowels explode in front of them? Or better still, I will demand a peacock . . . an opal . . . the philosopher's egg. That will give them something to discuss at their case meetings.

Where was I?

The bright chatter, the women's songs, are suddenly shouts and warnings as a bray of terror resounds across the bog. I fling away the yellow stars and race to where a crowd has gathered. Mary Margaret tries to follow, but her

41

mother's hand clamps her to the ground.

Crashing through the flurry of accusations, I stand on the edge of The Devil's Hole. The donkey's hooves are clawing at the bank, but the loaded creel drags him down again. When I take half a step forward, my father looms before me. The weight suddenly pulls the donkey backwards and, for an instant, I see him standing on the water, begging sugar like the pony in Mary Margaret's circus book. Then I see another donkey, its haunches raw from whipping, its dumb eyes bleeding on the perfect lawn.

How could I remember what? Jesus, you're so meticulous; so banal. Do you need to be a surgeon to know you have a heart?

My father's hand is on my shoulder, but how can I resist The Alchemy of Love? Can you stop yourself from thinking, or slow the blood rushing through your veins?

Like everyone else in Tonelemona, I have never learned to swim, but I know there is nothing to fear. Closing my eyes, I leap into the churning pool. My mother screams my name as I undo the belly-band and the creel sinks to the bottom. Gulping grotesque bites of air, the donkey jerks forward and attacks the bank again, but it just crumbles and he slithers deeper than before. His mouth shoots sparks of water through the sunlight until, at last, I manage to grasp his neck. Through a frenzy of hooves, my mother's cries, my father yelping for a rope, the words of love soothe their way into the donkey's ear.

With a shudder that leaves me floundering, he is safe on the bank. Shaking himself like a dog, he scatters the crowd and bares his teeth before galloping away across the bog. Someone pulls me out and, as I shiver among the cheers, I imagine the hind legs in the air like a bronco in The Widow Tynan's stories. My mother rushes forward and hugs me to her breast. She dries me with her knitting and, through the cacophony of tears, I try to catch what my neighbours are jabbering about The Mad Maneen.

Tell me this. Who, apart from anyone born different, suffers most from this black, vindictive world? It's the donkey. The poor humble ass. Why are you laughing? Do you know that poem by Chesterton? He knew the truth about the 'tattered outlaw of the earth'. No creature has ever shed more tears of blood. Even in this country, where he is as much a national emblem as the shamrock or the harp, you'll find his bag of bones tottering along laneways, peering wistfully through ditches. And yet we smile when he trots across a million postcards. How do you explain that? How can you torment any living thing, then make it the symbol of happy, carefree times?

I can't understand it. The donkey will work forever and be content to live on thistles. And his so-called obstinacy and stupidity . . . . What do you expect after centuries of cruelty and neglect? I will tell you something everyone on the bogland knows. There is no creature more naturally patient and persevering than the donkey. No creature with the same affection for its master. And I'll tell you something else. There is no creature closer to God. Who carried Mohammed into heaven? Who bore the sacred symbols through the streets of ancient Rome? Was he not present at the birth of Christ and rewarded with the star of Bethlehem on his forehead? Did he not bring Mary into safety in Egypt?

Did you ever bother to even look at a donkey? Did you notice the cross on his back? Where did that come from?

Some quirk of evolution? A coincidence of hair and pigment? Evolution! It is a gift from God because the donkey carried Jesus in triumph through Jerusalem.

And who suffered for my birth, and tried to save my infant life when the world refused to know me?

How can I remember anything when every time I try to think, Cesare and Lucrezia prod me with their questions. I am sick to death of their insidious smiles, their endless Why? When? How? pouring like Hamlet's leprous distillment in my ear. Lucrezia of the Deadly Hand; Cesare, Emperor of Guile; you plot in vain to snare The Alchemist of Love. I spit on you. I spit on all quacks, druids, witch doctors, medicine men and hags. My father was right. I spit on anyone who denies the glory of my life, and dares defile the sacred Rule of Love. I spit on all who timidly accept the dicefall of existence; genuflect before the notion that poverty, fear, pain, disappointment are dealt by the loving hand of God. To temper us, to make us 'better people'. The meek shall inherit the earth. An earth alive with worms. I spit on happiness hereafter. All my life, I tried to show that heaven can be here and now. Even in this mean provincial town. Through the magic of my hands, the simple alchemy of hands, I tried to bring healing to their lives. But they turned my love to hatred, flung it like turf mould in my eyes, and now, like John the Baptist, like Jesus, like all who bear the cleansing truth of love, I am made a scapegoat for my dreams.

All my life, I made The Rule of Love a light that shineth in the darkness, but the darkness comprehendeth it not. Why shouldn't I be angry? Who has suffered more from this accursed town?

A few days after she was four, Mary Margaret's father arrived home with a new dog: a snow-white Jack Russell with black eye-patches that The Widow Tynan immediately christened The Lone Ranger. It was probably rats Paddy Dunne had in mind, but, to his favourite daughter, Loney — unlike me, her infant tongue had limits — was a birthday present, and, from that day on, they were like Mary and her lamb.

One evening when my mother was collecting cotton on the bog, and I sat reading in the yard, my cousin beckoned me to the gate. As if on signal, my father's head appeared from the shed and warned me to go no further than Dunne's or the *dullahán* would get me. John promised to mind me and, just then, Mary Margaret came running towards us, her tears splashing the collar of her dress. She wiped an arm across her eyes, and ordered me to save him like I saved the donkey. Everyone knew, she said, that I had 'the gift'. I remember thinking how funny the word sounded from her lips.

Like children stealing eggs, we crept into Dunne's and opened the shed door. As if it was a prisoner waiting to escape, the smell swept past us into the yard. Huddled in a nest of straw, the dog looked dead. Mary Margaret whimpered that he had been like that all day, and her face dissolved in tears. I wiped the pus from its eyes and nostrils, cleaned the diarrhoea with a fistful of straw, and searched every part of me for the love that saved the kitten and the donkey.

Footsteps made me turn and I found the Dunnes looming in the doorway. When I asked Paddy to get me water, Mary Margaret jerked his hand and shouted in his face that 'Michael Joseph is going to make Loney better'. Closing my eyes, I willed the strength of love to permeate the wasted flesh. The Rule of Love hopeth all things. The Rule of Love never faileth. The words from my grandmother's Bible echoed in my head and when the shrivelled tongue touched the water on my finger, Mary Margaret's happiness made her parents cry.

I handed her the dog and as I ran from the yard, along the road that might suddenly erupt in blinding waves of blood, John's exultant cry — 'MIRACLE MICKEY! MIRACLE MICKEY!' — was the genesis of yet another legend that soared above the darkening midland sky; another fiction that would mesmerise the future and reverberate in a thousand baying voices around the whiteness of this room.

What do children fear the most? The dark? Their parents' anger? The eye of God the Father? Their guardian angel lurking at their shoulder?

None of these. They are frightened of being different to their peers.

At the age of seven, Chopin composed his Polonaise in G Minor. Emile Zola was abused by a servant and grew to hate all homosexuals. Perhaps you lean more towards the terpsichorean? Did you ever hear of Fred Astaire? Well, he was hoofing it in vaudeville at the same age.

So what? Didn't I tell you there is no such thing as useless information. You never know the time or place . . . . *Nam et ipsa scientia potestas est.*

At the age of seven, despite the magic of my hands, the million words that danced at my command, I was seldom happy.

The average height of a seven-year-old is fifty inches. I was thirty-four.

Seven what? I warned you never to use that word again. I am going to clear this up for once and for all. I'll tell you about dwarfs. Do you think all babies are born perfect? I could stiffen your hair with stories of human beings with heads no bigger than a billiard ball; creatures whose mouths could be silenced by the button on your shirt. There's 'freaks' for you. Will you snigger at that? Am I one of those?

Yes, I, The Mad Maneen of the bogs, will tell you all about dwarfs. I've studied the books; memorised every single word.

The most common type is the achondroplastic, which I needn't describe — you've laughed at them in the circus. The rarer type has perfectly proportioned limbs and body, but suffers from a deficiency of the growth hormone secreted by the anterior lobe of the pituitary gland. Is this my fault? Should my life be blighted by the whims of chemistry? Am I to be laughed at because my infant body harboured one malignant cell? Would you laugh at cancer?

The pituitary dwarf is small simply because he grows at a reduced rate, but he shows no deformity or mental deficiency. Look at Keats and Pope. Queen Victoria and Saint Francis of Assisi. The pituitary dwarf may be sexu— Where was I? In school? No, not yet. You can forget everything I've just told you. It's not important, and anyway, I made it all up. All I want you to remember is how much this poor

47

Zaccheus of the Boglands suffered for his lack of inches. As soon as I could stand, the other children mocked me. Even my parents' love caused embarrassment and pain. Witness my humiliation at the hands of Bartle Mooney. But they suffered too. My poor mother had to live with thirteen years of sympathy; thirteen years of prayers offered up for 'the unfortunate maneen'. Until the pennies locked them tight forever, my father's eyes were black with what even a child could see was hatred. Hatred for this town because it would not stop the tears he blamed for my inability to grow.

They say that, at the age of seven, the typical child first starts to challenge its parents. In this respect, at least, I was your typical child. I wanted to go to school; to be like Mary Margaret, three years younger, yet due to start in September. What did I do? How did I fulfil the prophecy of the paediatric textbooks?

I used the only weapon against which I knew my mother and father had no power. I started to cry. I wailed and bawled until they were moidered by the screaming ghost of Easter. In a matter of hours, my lungs achieved what Master Larkin, the priest, the police and The Mitching Man had been trying to do for years. And so, despite my age and mastery of words that ridiculed my years, my parents, in their determination not to have me different, started me in Ha'penny Babies alongside Mary Margaret.

On the feast of Saint Bartholomew, a week or so before I started school, the postman handed me a parcel addressed to Master Michael Joseph Purtock. My mother ordered me to open it myself. My father came and put his arm around her as I struggled with the twine and sheet after sheet of thick brown paper.

It is the smell I remember most. Even today, before I read any book, I open it in the middle and, like a priest bending to kiss the missal, hold it to my face. The sense of smell. Sometimes in the dead of night, when the drugs have this place snoring like a vast exhausted animal, I imagine lying on my deathbed. As I finally escape the clutches of this world, my soul rises through the scent of mother's milk and creosote; vanishes into darkness heavy with the smell of blood.

The sense of smell. Did you know that this town nearly murdered me with the sweetest smells you could imagine? No. Of course you didn't. But you've heard all about the monster I'm supposed to be.

Did you ever stop to think of all the people who have died since history began — faceless generations crowding the earth beneath your feet? Cities, deserts, mountains, bogs, all breathing the scent of the dead. Think of the food you eat; every grain, fruit and vegetable with its distinctive taste and smell. Every blade of grass . . . . What do you mean morbid? *Nihil humanum alienum est.* How else can we be part of all those gone before us?

The sense of smell. The tang of creosote. A room evaporates in creosote. They could abide everything else, even The Rule of Love, but they could not forgive the smell of creosote. It was creosote that brought them to The House of Love baying for my blood. Creosote that made them steal her from me when, after all those years of emptiness, she came back to me again.

What?

Nothing. I'm just talking to myself.

In what?

A thirty-volume set of *Great Classics of the World*.

I remember every detail precisely. Red imitation morocco, the titles embossed in gold. The minute stitching along the edges of the bookmark. The frontispiece whose tissue guard rustled when my excitement made me whistle. The end-papers like blobs of greenish water.

At first, my mother tried to convince me that Saint Bartholomew had brought a present for 'the best little boy in Tonelemona', but when my glance told her I was far beyond such fictions, she admitted ordering them from an advertisement in *The Midland Star*.

And so, while my future classmates ogled picture books, I sat for hours with Mary Margaret, entrancing her, making her love me all the more with the magic of my lips. On a raft of words that thrilled us with their strangeness, we sailed the Mississippi from the boglands. While the evening grew around us, I dealt Estella jacks and kings; felt her guardian loom behind us like a corpse. And when a sudden draught ruffled Mary Margaret's hair, I saw it whisper through the veils of lace, and blow that withered bride to dust.

Do you know what happened this morning? Cesare was tormenting me again when, out of the blue, he asked me why . . . . No, I can't repeat it. If Lucrezia had not stuck her face between us, I would have taken him by the neck and squeezed until his eyes hung on threads like the time the donkey stood on Nan-the-Habit's cat. But I am not a violent man. I cursed him for even thinking such a thing, and fell on the bed, whimpering until, for fear I would choke, they sat me upright. Black needlepoints swirled towards me and it was minutes, maybe hours, before I came to, rubbing my eyes and praying it was a dream.

Of course it was a dream. Jesus knows, no-one tried harder than the Purtocks to save Mary Margaret. My mother scoured the bog for bugleweed and traipsed through distant meadows in search of comfrey. She even broke a solemn promise to my father by going to town for creosote. Didn't we help Billy-the-Box with the gazebo? Who ever loved her more? Did I not close my eyes and wish my body drained of every breath that she might live? Did her wasted flesh not tremble at the love seeping from my hands? Am I not The Alchemist of Love?

I was so exhausted by their questions that I must have fallen asleep and it was all a dream, a ghastly nightmare. Or could it be the poison in the food?

Can you recall your dreams? Maybe so, but do you listen to what they say? Like all the world, do you hear them crying at how your life has disappointed them? I listen to my dreams. I hear them weeping for a life that tried to reach their highest expectations. I hear them weeping for a world that always let them down.

I have them in the palm of my hand. The Mad Maneen, Miracle Mickey of the playground, is now The Alchemist of Words. Perched on a stool before them, my words infiltrate their eyes and tell them what to see:

John's mouth hangs open as the village is attacked by fire from the sky. His gaze widens at little children torn by claws of flame.

Behind wire glasses, the witless eyes of Farmer Tierney ('Now, Tommy, what do we call God because he takes such care of all his creatures?' 'A farmer, Miss.') blink away tears as his new sister wriggles on the point of Herod's sword.

Mary Margaret leans forward in her desk and loves the boy who saved the drowning kitten.

Clowns tumble through the circus of her gaze, and Janey Lalor wobbles like The Fattest Woman in the World.

Mrs Clancy inches her tweed buttocks closer to the fire, her heart frozen by a scream of bells, the snapping of wolves at her careering troika.

But I swore that every word I am telling you is the truth, so I must admit that, despite my power, despite the awe in which the classroom held me (it was a different story in the playground), the four years I spent with Mrs Clancy were the longest of my life. When I wasn't perched on that stool, the minutes seemed to pass like hours. And no matter how I begged them, resorting to nights of tears that made them clutch the pillow in despair; no matter how I impressed them with my knowledge, my parents refused to let me jump forward into Master Larkin's.

I saw him ever day. Strolling through our lunch breaks, absorbed in the *Eclogues* or *Aeneid*, yet aware of every shout around him.

I was delighted when, on some errand or other, Mrs Clancy sent me to his room. Standing there, waiting for him to finish at the blackboard, my heart raced because I was familiar with every word he used. Toga. Hypotenuse. Plenary indulgence. Onomatopoeia.

The morning he put his arm around me, caressed my

cheek, and called me 'the renowned abecedarian'.

The time he lectured them on 'the obstacle of ignorance'.

'Delenda est Carthago! Delenda est Carthago!', he shouted at the window-panes, then suddenly turned and asked me if I knew what he was saying. Their sniggers made me stare at his boots, and, in their oxblood mirror, I saw the first evening he came to the cottage, my parents ignoring every word he said.

I could not wait to be in his class and, until I was eleven, I hated every day in school. That's not really true. I was just bored. Bored by Mrs Clancy and her strings of coloured spools; her chipped slates; the drawings I could surpass at three or four. Figures that slotted together without any effort on my part. Words that annoyed me with their ease.

After the first year or so, I could feel the others growing tired of what Mrs Clancy, with a smile that made me hate her, always introduced as 'another performance by the little man himself'. Until the day I left Second Class forever, it was only Mary Margaret that kept me from drawing The Mitching Man to the cottage again.

Hardly an hour went by but Mrs Clancy called Mary Margaret a fool. I will never forget how she made her stand in that corner, her poor face dirty with tears, until her quivering lips could chant the four times tables. I remember the morning she tried to pull her hair — I remember it so well because it was just after The Cropping. Did I tell you about The Cropping? Remind me again — and she screamed until the other children started crying too.

Why can I recall so little of my early education? Was it boredom, or my time with Mister Larkin, that robbed it from my memory? I don't know. Maybe I just don't want to remember, but, no matter how I try, turning the days like pages in the dark, only a few are visible with a clarity that is luminous:

Mary Margaret staring at figures that make her chew her hair.

Clouds through grimy windows. *Delenda est Carthago.*

Frost burning our feet on winter mornings.

Mary Margaret trembling in a corner, a black D pinned to her dress.

Mrs Clancy erect before the fire, steam rising from her skirt.

Master Larkin's hand.

The Renowned Abecedarian.

Mary Margaret and I, our cheeks touching when I unlock the mystery of a word.

A *danse macabre* in the playground. 'THE MAD MANEEN! THE MAD MANEEN!' Loney barking in delight. Mary Margaret pleading with them to stop.

What? I never told you that. I never mentioned anything about a wife. What need had I, The Alchemist of Love, of any carnal satisfaction? The Rule of Love must always stand alone. You're sure of what? Listen. Do you want the truth or not?

Do you like music?

When I built The House of Love, I had music in every room and, morning, noon and night, The Rule of Love was accompanied by the sweetest sounds you could imagine.

Gentle as the tongues of devils. Soft as whispers to the dying. Yes, I used to love music, but that all changed when they brought me here.

I can tolerate the old man I sometimes pass on the way to the toilet. Strumming his chest like a banjo, his cartoon voice squeaking that some day soon he'll fly away. He always stops me with the same question: 'Are you in here because you're not all there?' Then he makes a microphone of his fist and thrusts it in my face: 'Have you e'er a request for anyone in hospital? A special one for the best Mammy in the world?'

I can even put up with Lucrezia humming, Cesare tapping his knuckles with a biro. I have got used to all that, but what I can't stand is that caterwauling outside. Sometimes when I get tired thinking of the truth, I watch them through a slit in the curtains. The Men's Confraternity with banners of Saint Patrick, Saint Fintan, Saint Lazerian, covered in plastic bags against the rain. Do these people ever work at all? How do they know which room I'm in? From early morning, louder than guilds marching through a medieval nightmare, they shuffle back and forth, 'Faith of our Fathers', 'Soul of my Saviour' flung like stones against the window.

Children of Mary threatening me with rosary beads. 'Hail Queen of Heaven'. 'I'll Sing a Hymn to Mary'. Even a procession of little girls in Communion dresses, their gloved hands clutching matchstick drawings of THE MONSTER FROM THE BOG. Is this what they're learning in school? Listen to them! 'Tantum Ergo', 'Ave Maria'. A mockery of the grandeur that was Rome. Master Larkin, wherever you are today, wherever the quest for love has taken you, I am glad you cannot hear this travesty. Day and night, their squawking fills the grounds and terrifies the birds.

Every few days, a troop of women in boots and combat jackets marches up the avenue, rattling placards, bawling like strikers at a lorryload of scabs: 'SISTERS UNITED FOR THE EXPLOITED.' 'PURTOCK IS AN ANIMAL.'

Who has filled these strangers with such poison? The Rule of Love is patient and kind; it thinketh not evil, rejoiceth not in iniquity, but rejoiceth with the truth. They scream abuse until — and this happens every time — the choir starts up again. A porter threatens to call the police and everyone barks at everyone else until the military wing retreats, and the Sons of Saint Lazerian stamp the ground in geriatric triumph.

Why shouldn't I laugh? I laugh to keep from weeping at the hatred of this world. And, anyway, what distinguishes man from the beasts of the field but his ability to laugh? Am I not a man? Do you believe those placards too?

Yesterday I did cry. I cried until the sunlight blurred before my eyes. For the first time in months, there was someone who believed in me; someone who refused to bow before the evil of this town. I was watching through the curtains when this young man appeared with a guitar and stood beneath my window. And do you know what he was singing?

'Free Michael Joseph Purtock, the alchemist of love.'

It was as if I was back in my parents' bed again, so warmed was I by his words of love. But within minutes, in a welter of handbags and umbrellas, The Children of Mary were upon him. He tried to continue, but they hunched their shoulders and hissed at him like cats.

'Shame! Shame! Shame!'

'Shame! Shame! Shame!'

One old woman swung from his hair until she was dragged away by a red-faced member of the Confraternity.

Her husband, I suppose. They snarled and jeered as he walked backwards down the drive, his clenched fist punctuating words I could not hear.

Is it any wonder I cried? Tears of anger; tears of gratitude; tears of sadness for The Alchemist of Love. An outcast; despised by his own family, with no-one to defend him but some anonymous young man.

You find this amusing? Do you think my tears are only salt and water?

Why am I telling you this at all? Will you despise me too?

Where was I? Yes, music. Do you know where you will find the loveliest music of all ? On the bog, that's where.

There you are, laughing again.

Picture this:

It is a perfect summer's day. You are lying on the moneen and, two hundred feet above, a skylark is singing. No, this is not another hail to thee blithe spirit. What I am going to tell you will astound you with its truth; make you think again about the 'dullness' of the bogs.

For centuries, composers have pilfered from the throats of birds. I'm sure you have even pranced around some dance-hall to 'The Cuckoo Waltz'. Did you know that Haydn tried to imitate the clucking of a hen, or that Messiaen wrote a whole catalogue of bird music? So what? you ask. Composers are inspired by birds. Where does that leave your beloved bog? I will tell you where.

To define his territory, the skylark unleashes such a flood of song that no human ear could possibly assimilate it all. Even if you managed to record it, you would have to slow it down twenty times before you could distinguish every note. And what would you find then? Do you know the opening of Beethoven's Fifth Symphony? Of course you do, everyone does. Da-da-da-dom. Da-da-da-dom. The skylark's tune begins with a similar motif, and when Beethoven builds a theme from this, so does that speck fluttering high above you. The theme is developed, new ones created, and do you know what? The exact same thing is done by the Beethoven of the Boglands! The tiny creature you seldom even see follows the same precise rules of composition as Beethoven. What do you say to that?

Of course I'm serious. Didn't I tell you every word's the truth.

How do I know all this?

Simple. I spent years studying the natural music of the boglands. That's how. Modesty and, of course, professional ethics, prevent me from divulging the spectacular range of my research, but only to you, my undisbelieving friend, will I now reveal the most secret of my discoveries.

I forgot to mention that I also devoted years to the science of encephalology. Anyway, when I compared my work in both these fields, I could hardly credit the results. In the darkest, oldest regions of the human skull, deep beneath the cortex and the limbic system, I uncovered a tiny reptilian brain. And when I examined it, I found a system of organising sound identical in every aspect to that of birds.

What do you think of that?

What?

You can believe what you like.

Thirty seconds of the skylark's song fill forty pages of manuscript — eight minutes of music that would baffle the most accomplished performer. Now talk about your classics. Mankind's great musical heritage. Five-finger exercises the lot of them. In a lifetime devoted to music, Beethoven composed nine symphonies. Every day between dawn and dusk, the tiny syrinx of the skylark composes hundreds.

Mary Margaret was right. Everyone knew I had 'the gift'. And they were not slow to use it. Strangles. Laminitis. Seedy Toe. Coccidiosis. Newcastle Disease. Miracle Mickey cured them all. And hundreds more besides. Of course I was familiar with such words. Have you been listening to me at all? At the age of eight I was reading dictionaries like fairy tales.

You don't believe me? Ask me a word. Anything at all. The hardest you can think of . . . .

Late Middle English, from the Latin *superfluus*, running over. Excessively abundant or numerous. Needless. Uncalled for. A donkey would answer that. Look up something and ask me . . . .

What?

You're mispronouncing it. The emphasis is on the second syllable. A form of madness in which a man imagines himself to be a beast. Did you never hear of Buffalo Bill?

At ten years of age, I knew the precise scientific name for every ailment in Tonelemona. No, I certainly did not flaunt my knowledge. What need had I, The Alchemist of Love, to impress such simple people with my mastery of words? The old woman crying because her favourite hen refused to lay. Tom Fitzpatrick wondering why his poultice would not cure the donkey's foot. Joe Delaney embarrassed by the pus dribbling from his horse's nose. And, furthermore, I refused every offer of payment. Every bag of sweets from The Widow Tynan's. Every worn shilling pressed into my hand. The Rule of Love is not ambitious; it dealeth not perversely.

And so my hands became a legend. No wonder Bartle Mooney hated me. Who would traipse across the bog when I was in the village? Did I tell you he was here the other day? Spitting at the cameras that Purtock was the Antichrist. I could smell his breath from here.

Donkeys, horses, cows, fowl, dogs, cats, Joe Costigan's pet fox: my hands cured them all. I won't bore you with the details, but I want to tell you of the time I brought the village to the brink of civil war.

From the moment I was old enough to listen, I heard talk of Duckwings, Blackcaps, Redcaps and Spangles. When I questioned her, my mother snorted disapproval, and warned me never to follow my father and Uncle Joe in 'tormenting God's poor innocent creatures'.

Although it was declared illegal in 1849, cockfighting still flourished in Tonelemona, as in many other parts of the Midlands. Throughout the month of May, different townlands 'fought' each other, and the highlight of the calendar was the annual war between The Middle and The North. I can still see my mother with her back to the door, refusing to say goodbye as my father disappeared for the only nights he ever slept away from home.

But it was at a more local event that I caused uproar in the village. Picture this:

A circular pit, about six feet in diameter, has been dug inside the chapel walls. Chatting through drifts of blue tobacco smoke, the men are gathered round it. Occasionally their eyes dart to the corner where Flame is cradled in my father's arms. As he trims the comb and tail feathers, Uncle Joe's scissors flash stars of sunlight. In the far corner, Billy-the-Box is doing the same to Demon.

My mother is on the bog since dawn, gathering myrtle for her candles. I am perched with the other children on a mound of clay; laughing with them, but really wondering what she will say when I get home.

The referee calls 'Ready?' and the handlers fix the spurs. When he traces a cross in the air and Flame snaps at his fingers, my father grins and winks at Uncle Joe. I look beyond the greasy caps and The Lamb of God is dancing on the wall. In a cloud of feathers, he ascends towards Baby Jesus. My gaze follows him until the silver paten of the sun lacerates my eyes and he is gone.

The shouts draw me back to the pit, but again I turn away and think of Mary Margaret. The sickness that keeps her in bed on such a lovely day. I know she is always pale, but I know too that there is something wrong.

Suddenly my name is roared above the noise. My father is jumping up and down, teeth stripped like a dog, his mouth rimmed with blood. Behind him, Uncle Joe clutches Flame to his chest. My father spits a mouthful of blood into the crowd and waves his frantic arms.

'Miracle Mickey!' my cousin shouts, and the chant rises up around me: 'MIRACLE MICKEY! MIRACLE MICKEY! TIME TO BRING IN THE MAD MANEEN!'

Calling out my name, Uncle Joe holds Flame above his head, and I remember the day we spotted the hawk's nest. How I waited while he ran back to the cottage. How, stone by stone, he climbed the chapel wall, the precious egg wrapped in straw in the pocket of his waistcoat. How we watched like hawks ourselves until, one evening, he felt inside the nest and the walls echoed the whoops of his delight.

What? Must I explain everything? He believed the young cock would develop the ferocity of its adoptive parents.

My father bursts through the crowd, and drags me into the pit. 'Save him,' he spits.

Whatever he says next is smothered by the children: 'MIRACLE MICKEY! MIRACLE MICKEY!'

I am frightened by the smell of poteen, the threat of blood spewing from gargoyle mouths. The men suddenly break ranks and my mother is standing before me. She pulls me from the pit, lashes me across the legs and, as I stumble home before her, the scent of myrtle humiliates my every step.

The longer he was in the village, the more the mystery deepened. Why wasn't he married? Where did he go when he locked the school on Friday?

Tonelemona was not short of answers:

His wife was dying from cancer in some nursing home.

She was in the madhouse.

He was tending her grave in the town beyond the mountains.

He was visiting his seven children.

Pat Delaney spied him at the station and swore he had a woman in the city. The Zulu saw him leaving the hotel with two peroxide blondes.

Who?

Ah yes. Joe the Head. A naive master from the Midlands.

As a boy, he dreamed of making postcards from compressed turf. The village laughed, of course, but look today, everywhere you turn the shops are full of them. WARMEST GREETINGS FROM THE MIDLANDS. Mass-produced by some robot with a briefcase.

Is there no end to the exploitation of the Midlands? If I had some chic address, some Heights or Downs, do you think they would be hounding me today? I would be a national hero; cheered in the streets; celebrated in the papers. Instead, they are howling for my blood. Pillars of society whose wives once preened themselves before me; wore their ailments like jewellery; fought each other for the magic of my hands. If I wasn't from 'the wilds' of Tonelemona, do you think I'd be a prisoner here today?

How could Cesare say that about poor Mary Margaret?

Joe must be near a hundred now. When I was a boy, he was a withered little man as deaf as he was blind. Discovered by some tourist looking for directions, then swindled left right and centre by that gallery. A naive master from the Midlands.

He worked in oak collected by the villagers. Do you know about bog oak? How it lies beneath the ground, buried yet breathing for longer than the memory of the bog itself. How the artist, obedient to every nuance of its brittle voice, coaxes it awake with the softest touch of chisel, adorns it with the gentlest sand and beeswax.

When I built The House of Love, I used no timber but the blackest Tonelemona oak. I kept them busy for months, paid more than they dared ask for, and look how they thanked me. My own people. When I needed someone to defend me, they looked the other way.

Twice in their lives, on their tenth and fortieth birthdays, the villagers were sized by Joe the Head. It was during my final year with Mrs Clancy that, one crisp October morning, my mother led me through his gate.

The cottage had only two rooms. The first a storeroom for the oak and, despite his neighbours' protestations, a bedroom for the artist. For years, the men were offering to build another room, but Joe's refusal never changed: 'Sure if I don't watch them, they skedaddle in the night. Them heads is only bucking to get out.'

You had to go through that first room to get to the workshop.

What?

How do I know? Is it anyone else's business how you arrange your home? When I built The House of Love, I had some lackey from the Council whingeing about such and such a bye-law. Would I go to his house and complain about the goblins in the garden, the ducks squawking up his wall? *De gustibus non est disputandum.*

Where was I?

Yes. It was like entering the lair of some fabulous insect: a web of heliophobic branches gnarling from every corner into a canopy of claws. Or some prehistoric charnel house; mutilated torsos crowding the passage through which Joe's fingers led him to a squalid bed.

The heads hung on nails around the workshop: the full black images of the living, the hollow skulls of the dead. He put me sitting on a stump of oak and, as his hands explored my face, I scanned the walls until I found my parents. A single likeness of my mother; two of my father which, even in my innocence, made me shudder at the ravages of time. Each one hurts. The last one kills.

For an hour, his fingertips sought and registered the harmony of skin and bone, every filament of nerve and vein. I was trying not to think of Bartle Mooney when suddenly he straightened, scribbled something on a scrap of paper, and ordered my mother to come back in a month.

I can't remember why, but I never saw the result of his labour. I often wonder where it is today. Gathering dust in a corner of his workshop? Spat at, kicked through the streets like the head of some guillotined aristocrat? Or maybe Cesare, resorting to phrenology, has impounded it as 'evidence'?

Will I ever stand in that Golgotha a second time? Of course I will. When Cesare and Lucrezia tire of playing games; when justice has prevailed and I am restored to The House of Love, I won't have long to wait until his hands caress my face again. And what will they discover there? The scars inflicted by this accursed town? No. Living proof, throbbing from every pore, that The Rule of Love has triumphed over jealousy and pain.

Whenever someone in the village died, Joe Lalor was the first to be informed. Muttering prayers for the soul of the departed, he took the head and lovingly gouged out the eyes, mouth and nose. Every All Souls' Night, he inserted one of my mother's candles and impaled the heads on hazel sticks around the yard. And there, shivering in the aromatic dark, the entire village knelt before the orange grinning faces of their dead.

Have you ever stopped to think about the names imposed on you at birth? Are you happy being John, Mary, Thomas or Elizabeth? Would you rather be Patrick, Catherine, Margaret or Bill? I am serious. Some people go though life fighting with their names. From the time they learn to think, they are torn between who they are and who they want to be. How can such people ever be content?

What's in a name? I'll tell you.

On that clamorous Easter morning, I am sure my father clutched at the first one he thought of, and called me after

65

my grandfather. But this was much more than mere convenience. It was, in fact, the force of cosmic harmony. For, in the history of nomenclature, no-one was more aptly christened than yours truly. Michael Joseph. Was it not Michael who sent Satan and his cohorts hurtling like black stars to hell? Have I not spent my life locked in mortal combat with the powers of darkness too? In the East, Michael is venerated as a special guardian of the sick. Think of The Rule of Love.

Do you know that song 'Michael, Row the Boat Ashore'? Michael is no Caribbean fisherman, but the receiver of the souls of the dead. Have I not received the dead and restored to them the gift of life? What about the kitten in the barrel? Mary Margaret's dog?

Who do you think of when you hear the name Joseph? The carpenter from Nazareth? He was not the doddery greybeard of popular belief, but the very epitome of dignity and kindness. Need I say more? Think of Joseph of Arimathea, who rescued the body of Christ from Pilate. Did I not save her from the bog? And what about Joseph of Copertino? A frail, simple child, jeered at by society, yet devoted to the sick. There you are. The Mad Maneen. Miracle Mickey. And do you know something else? He could levitate at will. I am serious. Didn't I tell you every word's the truth? Some day soon, when I can bear this world no longer, I will close my eyes and, at the count of three, just like that old man's song, I will fly above this room; beyond the toxic gaze of Cesare and Lucrezia; high above the mob outside and this gaping midland town; higher and higher until I am a whisper in the air; a pure diaphanous angel forever guarding my beloved bogs.

When my mother started whitewashing the kitchen, I knew for certain my father was going to die.

Picture this:

It is the fifteenth of July, a blazing cloudless day. We are lying on our backs, wondering how such heat could last for forty days. Now and then, I lean towards Mary Margaret and lick beads of sweat from her forehead. Now and then, she opens her eyes and does the same to me. Can children be in love? What is love? All I know is my happiness depended totally on hers. Have you a better definition?

I ease away from her and scan the air for butterflies. I know she is pretending not to notice. That's love too. The Large Heath. Small Copper. Painted Lady. Red Admiral and Peacock. Mary Margaret loves them all. I want to trap one in my hand and kneel before her. I want to press her hands on mine, let her feel the beating of my heart.

A Common Blue hovers above a tussock, but before I can react, Loney barks and it ebbs into the sky. I turn around and she is smiling, her face paler than the Large White we followed through her father's garden. I am going to tell her how I want her for my sister, when the noise makes us jump.

The Zulu is attacking the donkey with a sprong. With every stab, it twists and turns between the shafts; skeleton's teeth chomping the air; a beard of froth erupting in drops of silver rain. When the cart takes off across the bog, The Zulu curses every donkey in the village and fires the sprong like a javelin towards the sun.

The men are huddled in the circle and, through a gap in their legs, I recognise the brown boots, the navy laces he laughed at when I brought them from The Widow Tynan's. He is lying on his back, a crimson thread trickling from his ear. Uncle Joe presses a rag to the far side of his head, but I just stand there, embarrassed that my father has wet himself in front of Mary Margaret.

I don't know how we got him home, but I remember waiting for the doctor.

My mother's brush slaps the kitchen wall and I picture specks of whitewash in her hair. Every few minutes, footsteps cross the yard and she roars at them to go away.

He is lying perfectly still, his startled eyes fixed on the ceiling. How can anyone stare so long without blinking? Why is there so little blood? Does Mary Margaret know he wet himself?

The door bursts open and my mother rummages in a drawer. Clothes I have seen only in magazines fly around the room, and when I go to snatch a nylon from my father's face, she snarls and holds a mirror to his mouth.

'What's keeping him?' she snarls again, and before I realise she means the doctor, she is gone. I stand beside the bed and clench my fists until they hurt; certain that my pain will summon up The Alchemy of Love. The Rule of Love believeth all things; hopeth all things, endureth all things. The Rule of Love never faileth. I touch the stubble on his chin and remember how he used to nuzzle me in bed. Tears force my eyes open. His are still the same. Fixed on something wondrous on the ceiling. Eleven years of love are pouring from my fingertips and my father never even blinks.

In the kitchen, my mother sits with the brush poised before her like a mirror. She mumbles something I can't hear, then springs forward and tears my father's otterskin from the wall. Rocking back and forth, she is suddenly the oldest woman in the village; crooning to that piece of skin, fondling it like a cat sleeping in her lap.

I run into her arms, and when I think she is going to kiss me, she just whispers 'You shouldn't leave your Daddy.'

She follows me back inside, telling me over and over 'Your Daddy's going to be alright.' His lips move and I believe her. His perfect words fill the room and I believe her.

'Clodcutters the whole bloody lot of ye.'

A grin seeps across his face and he starts to bray. My father starts to bray. A black hysteria of noise throbbing with the memory of blood that Easter morning.

'They wouldn't cure him, Mary! The bastards wouldn't cure the poor maneen.'

My mother covers her ears, but still it comes; shrieking through the history of The Mad Maneen; shrieking through the immanence of hands; the seven years I lay in this very bed; shrieking until she dances up and down, tearing her hair.

And then it starts to die, to shrink back inside the cavern of his mouth and, as we creep towards the bed, a single tear gathers in his eye. I have never heard such love as in the final words that dribbled from my father's mouth: 'I'm sorry, Neddy. I didn't mean it. Show me your poor eyes.'

He tries to lean forward, but there is a sound like water going down a sink and he collapses on the pillow. My mother flings herself across the bed, one minute stroking his face, the next pounding on his chest and, when I try to intervene, she hisses at me to go out and stop the clock.

I stand for ages on my father's chair, breathing in the smell of whitewash. I don't know what to do. To this day I still don't. How do you stop a clock?

What?

Yes, he came alright. Just when my father closed his eyes for good. Came and stood beside the bed, goading her for date of birth, full name and address, exact time of death.

This town abandoned me. It did the same to my father.

Like guns trained on my window, the cameras were back again today. When I went to draw the curtains, this foreigner raised a microphone and, to great amusement, shouted 'You lika the lezzer, no?'

The bastard. She was the most perfect creature I have ever seen, and when I carried her to my parents' bed, I could hardly breathe with the ecstasy of knowing she had come back to me again.

Every day I complain to Cesare about the noise. Sometimes he sends out a porter, but they are as alert as flies; vanished and back again the minute he's gone.

Lucrezia asks if I can talk of nothing but the bog. How can I? Behind every scrap of thought, every sound I utter, every word I write, there is sun, sky, solitude, stillness. Pervading my senses with the sibilance of wind.

For fear her tears might wake the Devil's dogs, my mother is sitting like a statue. I am staring at my father's treasure — the skull, arrowheads, strings of beads — trying not to hear the bare feet shuffling in the bedroom.

The door opens, the smell of myrtle fills the kitchen, and the women finally emerge. Nan-the-Habit nods once and a flood of tears makes my mother ugly. She squeezes my hand and leads me inside. When I ask why is Daddy upside down, she just cries all the louder.

What?

To avert misfortune, a man's head was always positioned at the foot of the bed. It symbolised the death of the family head.

When my eyes adjust to the gloom, his face is cleaner than I have ever seen before. Even Mary Margaret's cheeks have never been so white. I am frightened by his turf-coloured shirt, the pennies like black holes drilled through his head. As if she is reading my mind, my mother curses the women and plucks the pennies from his eyes.

In 1821, the Lenten Regulations for our diocese forbade 'unseemly behaviour' at wakes. Mourners, the bishop decreed, should enter the house of the dead *tremore et reverentia* . . . .

Poteen has materialised from somewhere and the cottage is dense with tobacco smoke and sweat. I have been given the job of filling the Lord-have-mercy pipes and handing them to the villagers as they enter. They touch the black diamond on their shoulders and whisper the traditional response: 'He's a great loss so he is. May the Lord have mercy on the souls of the dead.'

Mary Margaret is standing under my father's eel-spear. Her eyes are red, and a warm feeling tells me it is my grief that makes her weep. Yes, children can be in love.

From the shed where I once stood mesmerised by shafts of golden light, Billy-the-Box's hammer punctuates the revelry outside. Children yell and chase each other through the yard; young men and women have started 'Steal the Soul from Hell'. Do you know it? This is how it goes: Tim Delaney is standing in a circle, a sod of turf in each hand. When they count to three, he extends his arms and legs, then falls forward, balancing on the turf and the toecaps of his boots. Someone rolls a potato, and he tries to catch it in his mouth, all the time keeping his body from the ground.

'What are you doing?' the circle calls.

'Stealing a soul from hell.'

'Who owns the soul?'

'It's the soul of Straightface Purtock.'

'Swear it is.'

'I swear it is.'

Yes, despite that bishop and Saint Paul's injunction to the Thessalonians, our village revelled in its mourning.

I turn from the yard and listen to the keeners in the wake-room. First they recite my father's genealogy, then a lullaby of incidents from his childhood. Rising in a litany of his love for his family, his kindness to neighbours, his prowess on the bog, the women's voices split the tainted air.

The wail is taken up by my mother and everyone in the house until suddenly it stops in mid-air. They begin a low operatic chant that brings goosepimples to my arms.

'Who'll warm the home with you in the ground? Who'll warm the home with you in the ground?'

Men slap the rhythm on their thighs, feet pound the floor until it seems the cottage will explode with the sadness in their hearts. When I glance at Mary Margaret, she is staring at me, her hands clapping beats of love that reverberate in my throat.

Do you know the old saying 'Sing a song at a wake, shed a tear when a child is born'? Tonelemona never knew such music as when my father died. All that night, the silence of the bog was banished by a fiddle scratching jigs, reels and polkas, Master Larkin's recitations, the singing from the yard.

Just before midnight, someone shouts 'Himself is here', and the children run inside. Jim Malone leaps from the ground and flings the potato into the ditch.

When the priest enters the yard and my mother runs to kiss the biretta, I can see the disapproval in his eyes.

In the wake-room, he scatters holy water on my father and gives out the first decade of the rosary. The minute he is finished, he nods to my mother and sidles through the door. Why did he come at all? Was it the load of turf, the promise of devotion my father offered him that Easter? Who knows? But a mumbled Our Father, Hail Marys, Glory be to the Father, and he is gone.

My mother is followed by Uncle Joe and, according to custom, Master Larkin. '*Pater noster, qui es in coelis*', he begins, then suddenly stops in embarrassment. Not even on the night I tore his books to ribbons did I see such colour in his face.

What?

Nothing. We had a row over Virgil. That's all.

He mutters an apology and starts again in English, each syllable so perfect that the responses sound like a foreign language.

When my turn comes, I can feel his eyes on mine. I am so filled with pride, I have to concentrate on words I know by heart. But there is something else in his gaze; something I can't understand.

The prayers have ended and everyone leaves the room

except the family. Uncle Joe takes my hand and tells me to 'Say goodbye to Daddy'.

My lips touch his marble face and my body tenses with The Alchemy of Love. I saved the kitten, the donkey, hordes of useless animals, but I am powerless now. The magic trembles for an instant and seeps away like pain.

I run from the bed, through the startled faces in the kitchen, past Billy-the-Box standing like a sentry beside the upturned coffin. If The Widow Tynan had not stopped me, I swear I would have raced across the bog, my fists raging at the moon; cursing my father, my mother, Mary Margaret, the useless Alchemy of Love.

Outside, the men are lighting torches and each child is handed a *geataire*, a splinter of bog deal whose symbolic flame will die before they reach the gate.

Picture the scene:

Billy-the-Box shouting orders as my father is bumped through the door. Shadows dancing on the whitewash. Mary Margaret finding my hand as the cortege leaves the house and crawls towards the graveyard.

What is the last word you will ever speak? Think about it. Does the thought frighten you? Will it be said in terror . . . joy . . . anger . . . resignation?

I want to die suddenly. I want my soul to slip away. My soul. What is the soul? I'll tell you what. Peel away the layers of mumbo-jumbo; forget your eschatology, and it is nothing more than the memories you have accumulated in a lifetime; the memory you leave behind when you are gone. Memory. That's all. No more. No less.

Did my father's soul crumble into countless shreds of sound; syllables ascending through the air like feather-weights of ash? Did they sail beyond the faces at his bed-side, through the walls of the cottage, above the bogs he loved, the town that filled his heart with pain? Through the burning air, through time, through the past? Did they float above the regions of the dead, pleading for all the Purtock voices gone before him?

Did they vanish through the future? Will they ever merge again; congregate in words of rumour, words of local legend, words of endearment in the mouths of those who loved him? Words among strangers, who, learning of his death, learn for the first time of his existence? Or did he just die? All I know is my father will never speak to me again.

And still the animals kept coming. I must have cured Francy Costigan a hundred times. Did I tell you about Francy?

Shortly after I was born, Joe found him in a ditch, licking his mother's frozen mouth. He brought him home, reared him like a pup, and, all through my childhood, he was a celebrity in the village. He was even famous in the town where the two of them often stayed for weekends.

In the beginning, Francy performed *au naturel*, but when someone suggested he might look better 'dickied up', Joe persuaded Mrs Dunne to make a costume. A satin waistcoat with F embroidered on the back; baggy white trousers; blue beret; snow-white slippers with tinkling silver bells and matching pristine gloves.

They would install themselves in The Widow Tynan's and, from every glass bought for Joe, a drop was poured into a thimble. Francy would stand on his hind legs, take it in his magician's paw, throw back his head and drink it like a man. Then he'd bark twice and extend a paw for more. If nothing was forthcoming, he'd leap on Joe and drape himself as lifeless as a fur around his neck. But if there happened to be music — a fiddle, say, a *bodhrán*, even Joe's discordant lilting — he'd gulp the poteen, stretch both paws above his head and dance a hornpipe faster than a drunken sailor.

It was usually on Monday mornings that Joe arrived with Francy comatose in his arms. When I stroked the brittle fur, one eye would open and roll around for a minute before settling on his master. My mother used to scold me for wasting my gift on 'such a useless yoke', but she was wrong. Are not five sparrows sold for two farthings, and not one of them forgotten before God?

One morning in November, Joe arrived later than usual. I was at home because Master Larkin had not arrived to open the school. ('Where is he this time?' the village wondered, its eyes filled with blondes.)

'Would you be able to throw an eye on the oul' shanks?'

Before I could reply, he had rolled up his trousers, exposing milky flesh gnarled with veins. As if it belonged to someone else, he lifted the leg and offered it to me.

My hands had failed my own father, why should they work their magic now? But Joe's phlegmy groans, the pleading in his bloodshot eyes, made me kneel before him.

Whenever I met him afterwards, he embarrassed me with praise for the wonders I performed. In The Widow Tynan's, Francy raised his thimble to long life for Miracle Mickey, his paws dazzling in a jig for the genius of my hands.

But tragedy was lurking in the wings. Tragedy in the shape of politics. It was during an election in town that someone spiked Francy's poteen. In the middle of a horn-pipe, he suddenly collapsed and lay flat on his back, grinning at the ceiling, the empty thimble still twitching in his paw. In the uproar, he somehow disappeared — was his tongue presented for five shillings at the barracks? — and, early next morning, Joe staggered home, his swollen eyes fixed on the tiny slipper held before him like a lamp. Even harmless animals could not escape the malice of this town. What chance had The Alchemist of Love?

Lucrezia's notebook lies open on the desk. A single sentence is dramatised by three baroque question marks. Have you ever tried to read something upside down and backways? It is not easy, but word by stolen word, I pieced it all together.

'Between twenty and thirty per cent of all children who are physically or sexually abused do not grow normally.'

At birth I measured thirty inches. Was I molested in the womb? The fools!

The what?

Ah yes, The Cropping.

On the first morning of each new year, the women of Tonelemona queued outside Paddy Dunne's cottage. One by one he let them in and, twenty minutes later, they emerged into the shivering yard, their hair cut to just below the ear. For days after, the smell of something human lingered in our nostrils.

Here's a story for you:

Early on New Year's morning 1577, Patrick Dunne kissed his wife and infant daughter, and set out for the Hill of Mullaghmast. As Captain's hooves clattered through the frozen lanes, he wondered what the English would propose this time. Would it end the days of rumour, plots, and bodies found in ditches; nights of dreading every footstep on the road?

At the foot of the hill, a cloud of breath rose above the tethered horses. Not even at the Easter Fair had he seen so many animals assembled. He dismounted, led Captain to the picket-line and climbed through the icy trees.

The rath — a grassy hollow in the summit, about two hundred feet across — is filled with men from every corner of the Midlands. When Sir Andrew Harpoll fires his pistol in the air, a hush filters through the crowd. They await his welcome but, instead, shouts come from below, followed by a thundering of hooves. A hundred musketeers appear on the ridge and suddenly the air is thick with gunpowder. A ring of pikemen bursts from the trees and charges down the slope.

Patrick Dunne claws his way into a mound of bodies and, all that treacherous morning, cowers there in the darkness, his lungs screaming for gulps of fetid air. He sees Mary crooning to his daughter. He sees her crouched above him, her eyes wild, her hair cascading on his naked chest. He sees her waiting by the window for Captain's clip-clop on the lane . . . .

When the jeers have faded in the distance, he squirms into daylight and, for a moment, stands dazed by the innocence of birdsong. He runs, falls, picks himself up and runs again towards the trees. Clutching at roots, torn by frost and briars, he tumbles down the hillside.

Snorting flecks of blood, a white horse staggers towards him, a sword embedded in its flank, a hooded crow triumphant on its head. He blinks and it is gone.

The history books tell us that no-one escaped from the massacre of Mullaghmast. They are wrong. Patrick Dunne, leader of the village of Tonelemona, lived to tell the story and, for the remainder of his life, wished to God he hadn't.

It is dusk before he stumbles into the village. There is no-one there to greet him. No-one to enquire what happened Captain, or why he has been so long; no breathless queries about a historic new agreement. Patrick Dunne reaches his cottage, and there is Mary hanging from the elders, her naked body slit from throat to groin. And there is his daughter hanging from her mother's hair.

By the age of eleven, eight per cent of all boys will have had their first ejaculation; four per cent a deepening of the voice. The average height is fifty-nine inches. I was forty. Beethoven became a professional musician at eleven. John Evelyn began his famous diary. Buffalo Bill was a mounted messenger in Kansas. William Penn saw God. The Mad Maneen went into Master Larkin's.

I was so happy I didn't care if my classmates mocked my lack of inches or the years that separated us. I didn't care if, in the eyes of Tonelemona, I was 'neither hay nor straw'.

No longer was my knowledge deemed outlandish. No longer did I have to quell the words that danced upon my tongue. When I marvelled at Frank Lloyd Wright's plan to build a mile-high building in New York; a rapier of steel teeming with a hundred thousand workers, Master Larkin's eyes followed mine to focus on the heavens.

He cleared his throat and nodded in agreement at my tale of Fabius, choking to death on a single goat-hair in his milk.

His boots tapped in rhythm as I told them of the dancing plague that devastated Europe. Shrieking, moaning, tearing their hair, frothing at the mouth, a million manic dancers whirling from one village to the next. Of course I'm serious. The Church even organised pilgrimages to combat the disease.

Only once did he ever try to stem my cataract of words. That was the morning I began the strange saga of Napoleon's little penis.

'Hurrying from the Acmonian Wood?' he used to smile when I arrived hand-in-hand with Mary Margaret.

'Youthful Acacetus' he called me when I ran out of astonishing things to say.

When he stroked my cheek, I was always his Adonis.

He knew how much I missed my father, and every word, every gesture, every touch of his hand, was designed to ease my pain. He loved the others too, but I was the special one, his golden child, his *primus inter pares*. He gave me books from his own library (on the day of his arrival, two carts were needed to carry it to the cottage), and he never appeared on Monday morning without a present for his 'voracious little bookworm'.

I didn't realise it then, of course, but he possessed that rare ability to convey the absolute truth, the priceless value, of what he had to say. I, too, have been blessed with this power. My success in five continents speaks for itself.

Never knew what?

How could you? Do you think the papers would waste their precious column inches on a bogman? Now, of course, it is different. Like starving curs, they have descended on the village, devouring my success, spewing it out in poison that keeps me here today.

Master Larkin gave me more than Literature, History, Geography, Curiosity, Mathematics. (How Mary Margaret's eyes used to flutter at the shifting alphabet of Algebra.) I left his school with more Latin than the Pope. I knew all of Shakespeare, and the legends of twenty different countries. I had more understanding of humanity, more awareness of The Alchemy of Love than Cesare and Lucrezia find in all their years of gazing into people's thoughts.

My years with Master Larkin should have been the happiest of my life. But as flies to wanton boys are we to the gods. They kill us for their sport.

I never stopped thinking of my father.

Day after day, I roamed the bog; touching banks of turf he had cut; searching for his footprints in the muck. I went each week to tend the myrtle bush my mother planted on his grave. I padded to her bed at night and fell asleep with my tears drying on her face.

Whenever she went out, I took his eel-spear from the wall and, running my thumb along its three serrated blades, closed my eyes until his stories filled the dark. I saw him wave a torch above The Devil's Hole. I saw the dazzled heads surrender to his spear. I heard the death screams of his Uncle Joseph, poisoned by their blood. I spat out the lumps of eel cheese his mother forced upon him. I saw a million eels sliding from a bog-hole, their bodies silvered by moonlight as they journeyed home to die.

That spear became the central icon in my life. I loved it as other children love their father's memory card; the dying echo of his voice; the trace of sweat that lingered when he kissed them goodnight.

Of all the images that jostle in my mind, only two are brighter than the thread of blood that killed my father.

Mary Margaret crying beneath that eel-spear at his wake.

Mary Margaret gaping at the stars, her nightdress steeped in blood.

Were you ever tormented by happiness, so besotted by well-being, that your life became a misery? When Mary Margaret loved me, I used to lie awake at night; every thump of my heart, every bead of sweat, a warning that some day I might lose her.

We were inseparable. We used to huddle at the fireside, whispering to each other the words I had found in a seventh-century poem: 'As the donkey follows her foal, may your love follow my face from today until the day I die.'

We would walk hand-in-hand for miles; she teaching me the ways of butterflies; me pulling stories from the air. She never stopped praising the magic of my hands. I pestered her about the mysteries of her parents' bedroom.

I loved her so much I hated anything that came between us. Her parents, her brothers and sisters, even butterflies. But most of all I grew to hate her dog. I hated his name — imagine calling anything Loney! — his joyous yapping, his silly tricks that made her squeal. I hated him like a rival when she insisted on bringing him on our walks. I hated his nose that poked beneath her dress and was rewarded with a puckered kiss. I hated the fur that warmed her body; the paws that clambered over her; the stupid eye-patch that made her love him all the more.

Do you know what I did this morning? Just for fun. Just to shorten the day. I started howling that there was something in the wardrobe. Something fierce that wanted to get out and maul me. When Lucrezia unlocked the door, I fell on all fours and snarled like the fifty hounds of Actaeon. I snapped at her ankles and clawed the buttons from her coat. 'Down Mr Purtock! Down I say!'

You would think she was talking to a dog. I drooled until she locked the door again, and when she reappeared with Cesare, spitting 'Lycanthropy! Lycanthropy!', there was yours truly, curled like a kitten on the bed.

Before I reached my thirteenth year, The Rule of Love had saved Joe Costigan, Mattie Farrell, Ann Delaney and her daughter Mary.

It was only when Mag Fitzpatrick sent for me that I finally realised why my mother would never sit inside the cromlech. And who could blame her? Should she risk again the agony of that Easter morning? Barren women were shunned in Tonelemona and, for seven years, Mag endured the searching eyes, the nights stretched within the stones that tradition swore would make her fertile. Nine months to the day after she was blessed by my hands, her good news spread like bad news through the village.

All morning, while the women made the Biddy Cakes and wove the crosses that would protect the thatch from lightning, we were busy with our patron saint.

Now, mounted on a stick, she is ready, her white dress fat with straw, her head a turnip crowned with cotton tresses. There is no whingeing over who should bear Miss Biddy on her journey. Mary Margaret is the most popular girl in the village. Everyone loves her. And she has never loved anyone but me.

Because it is the first wild flower to herald her feast-day, the dandelion is special to Saint Brigid and, so, Mary Margaret's hair is radiant with its yellow suns. She raises Miss Biddy above her head and we set off along the lane, forty voices chanting through the January air:

> Here is Brigid dressed in white,
> Give us a penny for her delight.
> She is deaf, she is dumb,
> She cannot talk without a tongue.

All that afternoon, we march from house to house until, as darkness falls, we crowd into Dunne's yard and count the money for the Pattern.

For longer than anyone can remember, Saint Brigid's Day has been celebrated in Tonelemona. In the twelfth century, Giraldus Cambrensis wrote about the festivities he encountered here. He was especially fascinated by Saint Brigid's fire — the perpetual flame enclosed by a hedge and strictly out of bounds to men.

How could it what?

What's the point in explaining? You won't believe me anyway.

Picture this:

It is early afternoon and the noise from the bawnogue flies for miles across the bog. Tom Fitzpatrick's fiddle and The Widow Tynan's poteen have the villagers prancing like fools. Young lads ogle bobbing breasts; children belch lemonade and imitate their parents' feet. Away in a corner, two old men are waltzing cheek to cheek, their eyes pious with concentration. The fiddler is sawing like a dervish. 'The Copperplate'. 'The Lads of Laois'. 'The Bucks of Oranmore'. Not even on the night we buried my father did I see so many people drunk.

Someone calls for Master Larkin, and the women sing his name until he steps into the green. When he whips off his coat and throws it in the air, I run to catch it and hold it in my arms; savouring his warmth, the aroma of his sweat.

He rolls up his sleeves and suddenly his red boots are flashing to 'The Maids of Tonelemona'. A roar greets his response to every grace-note; how his body follows every scrape of Tom Fitzpatrick's bow.

'Will you look at the grand cut of him.'

'Maybe that's what he does be doing at the weekends?'

'God, he's only built for love.'

'Twelve inches of it.'

'Nora!'

'And from what The Zulu saw at the hotel, he doesn't be using it as a rule.'

'Nora!'

The women's laughter merges with the shouts for more, but Master Larkin bows like a suitor in a pantomime and slips back into the crowd.

Husbands shout for someone else's wife, boys leer at sweaty girls, and the entire village joins arms for the Biddy Dance. A gap opens and, Miss Biddy poised above her, regal

Mary Margaret walks into the ring. *Et vera incessu patuit dea.* Her proud eyes follow mine as round and round I go, still clutching Master Larkin's coat.

The voices reach the chorus —

> Welcome to the Queen of Spring.
> Come bless us now as we all sing . . . .

— and suddenly Mary Margaret crumples to the ground. In a flurry of straw and cotton, Miss Biddy topples from the stick. Her head rolls along the trampled grass, slower, slower, and slower, until her gouged eyes are gaping straight at me.

She cried all the way from Bartle Mooney's. She is still crying as she tells me about it now. His breath that corrupts the air when I remember him. The hazel twitching on her naked chest. Her parents' threats when she keeps insisting that she's never hungry.

Her life is making Mary Margaret weep. Cod liver oil shovelled through her lips. Vegetables spilling from her clenched teeth. The trace of arsenic in the food she spits across the table. Drops of creosote stirred into her milk.

Her body shudders again and I lick the tears from her face.

Poor Mary Margaret. The tang of creosote on your lips.

The Sons of Usnach. Homer and his winedark sea. Dante and Beatrice. Socrates and hemlock. Virgil's bees and cattle. He might as well be talking to the dead. Even when he crushes into her empty seat beside me; even when he strokes my thigh, I can only smile like someone at a graveside. Those should have been the happiest days of my life.

One night when her coughing kept the villagers awake, Paddy Dunne hammered on our door. I could hear him crying in the kitchen. My mother told me to get dressed and it was still half-black as I followed her, peering into ditches for brooklime, wading through unfamiliar meadows for the rosé spikes of comfrey. Traipsing over miles of bog for the love of Mary Margaret.

As the sun found chinks in the curtain, I fell asleep to the sound of chopping, grating, pounding; water bubbling in a saucepan.

What?

Of course they did. They had a path beaten to the town. They spent days wandering like beggars from hospitals in the city. And what were they offered? A bed in some distant sanatorium. In six months' time! Would you let your own flesh and blood suffer away from home? My father was right. What did they care about some peasant's daughter from the boglands? And do you know what one of them said? Some sex-fiend with a stethoscope. She was experiencing a traumatic passage into puberty; when her period became regulated, she would show immediate improvement! What do you think of that?

I spit on the Hippocratic trade. Yes, my poor father was

right. What can we expect from the town?

Cesare says they are having a meeting tomorrow to 'review my progress'. Progress towards what? The fools. *Parturient montes, nascetur ridiculus mus.*

It was children searching for a wren that came upon her. Stretched on my father's grave, her arms clenched around the myrtle. They ran to Joe Delaney's and he carried her home. Through the kitchen hot with cradle cakes and the goose she had left me minding. Into the bedroom where, an hour before, she had coaxed me awake with kisses and handed me *A Thousand Wonders of the World.*

When Nan-the-Habit prised open my mother's fingers, the smell of myrtle hurt my eyes like smoke.

On Saint Stephen's Day, when the village should have marched behind the king of birds, my father's grave was opened. That night, instead of joining in the songs that made her think of him, she went to sleep with him forever.

What killed my mother?
  Was it a broken heart?
  The miles she traipsed for Mary Margaret?
  Mary Margaret's bones?

Was it the ghost of Easter?
My father's death?
His hatred of the town?
Was it the *pooka*?
The *dullahán*?
Was it The Rule of Love?
Miracle Mickey?
The Mad Maneen?

Imagine every shred of vegetation that made the Midland Bog. Every sod of turf harvested by centuries of slanes. Think of all the prayers said for me that Easter. All the tears my parents wept. Every sound uttered since creation. Count the bristles on your face. The stars in the sky. Every breath you have ever taken. How many cells are in your body? All it needs is for one to go wrong. Is death such a mystery after all?

At fourteen years of age, eighty-two per cent of all boys will have ejaculated; ninety-two per cent developed pubic hair. Regarding the former, my experience was zero. Regarding the latter, I awoke one morning and found a single thread curling from my left testicular area. Day and night for a week, I observed this phenomenon, then, another morning, I searched and it was gone. Every time I see Lucrezia's mole, my fugitive filament comes back to me again.

Trailing their black spoor, they arrived again this morning. Old women fat with woollens, picking out their husbands' footprints. Banners held like shields against the snow. Despite their muffled faces, I recognised the banker and his wife. That bitch started it all. No. Why should I be angry? Anger is the mark of the defeated. Am I defeated? Am I broken by the hatred of this town? Soon I will be vindicated, restored in glory to The House of Love. And what of them? They will be forgotten. All the muckraking, the pious cries of outrage, every sanctimonious prayer: gone like snow off a ditch.

As I watched, a snowball burst against the window. They have even poisoned little children. Look at them. Their gloved paws threatening me with First Communion prayer books. If it wasn't for The Rule of Love, would some of them be here at all? They would still be shadows. Shadows screaming to escape a barren womb.

Before my uncle boarded up the cottage, I spent a morning rooting through my parents' past. My father's treasure. His eel-spear. My mother's clock. A box of myrtle candles. The picture of my mutton-chopped relations. I packed them in a tea-chest and, gulping back the tears, carried them next door.

In a drawer, tucked beneath her underclothes, I came upon a bundle of letters. With wayward fingers, because I knew I was exhuming something she had taken to the grave, I untied the string and, one by one, found twenty identical letters addressed to doctors in twenty different towns.

Despite the tinker woman's bugleweed and all the cures my mother left behind, Mary Margaret was often so weak we would gather round her bed, our voices alternating in the special prayer for the sick:

> Christ walked in a rocky place.
> A donkey's foot was hurt.
> He put blood to blood.
> Flesh to flesh.
> Bone to bone.
> As he healed that, may he heal this.
> Amen.

I hated sleeping with my cousin. I hated the smells he made; the things he asked about Mary Margaret; his stories about the women in the shop; the way the bed jumped when he thought I was asleep. Realising that he was 'never cut out to be scholar', Uncle Joe had apprenticed him to a butcher in the town and, from the day I went to live with them, all I heard from John was blood. Blood and women.

One Sunday morning I was called into the yard. John, my uncle announced with pride, was going to give us all an 'expedition'.

Picture this:

On a scoured table, surrounded by our neighbours, Joe and Auntie Annie are holding the barrow on its back.

'There'll be no waste here,' he laughs, 'that young lad'll make tin whistles with the squeal.'

John emerges from the shed, his long knife slicing air in a showman's flourish for the girls. With a lavish bow, he acknowledges their applause. Then he turns and his fingers caress the flabby neck. When he has found his spot, the knife flashes in a silver arc. I close my eyes and see The Lamb of God tearing at his collar of blood. Screams lacerate the cheers and, when I look again, John's hands are bloody to the elbows.

They immerse the carcase in a tub of steaming water, then drape it across a saw-horse to scrape off the bristles.

'No hairy bacon for the Purtocks', my uncle gloats, and again John winks at the girls.

As if I was three or four again, terrified by my father's armoury of slanes, I would not go near the shed for days. Entangled with my dreams of Mary Margaret, I saw that carcase hanging from the rafters, a potato rammed into its mouth; the plop of blood into the basin I would never use again.

With bits and pieces gathered from the neighbours, we built the gazebo — a slanting roof on four fencing posts — where, on summer nights, Mary Margaret might breathe miraculous wafts of air.

He asked me to stay back one evening and help him with the Maybush. It was too wet to work outside, so we set it up in a corner of the classroom and decorated it with eggshells we had kept and painted through the year. Out of the blue, he started telling me about his life. His native town across the mountains. All the schools he had known before he came to us. When I asked why he moved around so much, he laughed at his wanderlust; how he liked to be 'peripatetic just like old Aristotle'. But of all the children he had ever known, none made him happier than his class in Tonelemona.

When he asked about Mary Margaret, his face went redder than his boots. I could hear the shells rustling on the Maybush. He said I was still very young; there would be plenty of time for girls when I 'assumed the *toga alba virilis*'.

I was tying a ribbon when his breath exploded on my neck. 'O Adonis, my Adonis', he wept, crushing me with love, squeezing from my heart the horror of my parent's death, the tragedy of Mary Margaret.

With the bone clenched in my fist, I steal past the sleeping cottage.

The potions, the embrocations, the endless prayers and relics, even the magic of my hands, have all been futile. But I know this time will be different.

When his jaws flash open, I throw the bone and, dancing like a lamb, he disappears into the elders.

She is on her back, still as an effigy on a medieval tomb.

93

Her head makes no impression on the pillow. The Rule of Love never faileth. When my fingers trace her blue lips, the magic thunders in my blood. The Rule of Love never faileth. Her eyes flutter and she starts to twitch as if recoiling from a nightmare. She throws her arms around my neck and pulls me down. The smell of creosote hits me like a drug. My father, my mother, The Mad Maneen, the ghost of Easter, evaporate in creosote. The world evaporates in creosote.

Then I hear her voice . . . .

She is telling me to go away. She is tired and wants me to go home. I lay my hands upon her and she starts to cry: 'Daddy Daddy.'

My mouth touches hers and the tang of creosote is fire on my lips. Her head shakes violently and she pushes me away. As if a wall of flame suddenly roars between us, I turn and scramble through the yard.

Is it any wonder she refused The Alchemy of Love? For months she had suffered every sort of degradation. Eat this. Drink that. Do this. You can't do that. Doctors poking every part of her. Mooney's toxic breath. Even my own hands. Is it any wonder all she craved was sleep? A little folding of the hands to sleep. Dreamless uninvaded sleep.

I don't know how to tell you this, but I must. I promised you the truth. The Widow Tynan was picking wild raspberries for the shop. . . . No. I can't. I can't. The words refuse to come. I'll read you something. It was an editorial in *The Midland Star*. For twenty years I have carried it with me like a relic.

The entire Midland region is in a state of profound shock following the horrific death of little Mary Margaret Dunne, twelve-year-old daughter of Patrick and Mary Dunne of Tonelemona. This terrible deed, which police are treating as murder, occurred during the early hours of Sunday last, July 27th. The most pathetic aspect of this ghastly affair is that the dead child was an invalid, suffering from a chronic wasting disease. Such was the gravity of her condition that, during the summer months, she was accustomed to sleeping outdoors in a specially constructed gazebo so that she might benefit from the open air. Words cannot express our revulsion at this heinous crime, and we can only hope and pray that its vile perpetrators are swiftly brought to justice. To her grieving family and friends we extend our most heartfelt condolences.

For the first time in my life, I knelt beside the bed each night, my fingers clenched in supplication: *De profundis clamavi ad te, Domine; Domine, exaudi vocem meam.*

How could anyone endure such a trinity of heartbreak? A few short years had robbed me of everyone I loved. If it wasn't for Master Larkin, I would have gladly followed them myself. In the black of night I would have welcomed the silent alchemy of death. Only for him, I would have gorged myself on the arsenic left behind by Mary Margaret. I would have taken my father's eel-spear, planted it upright in the ground, and forced my throat against its triple blade, down, down, down, until my frantic arms were still. Only for him, I would have driven the world from my eyes and plunged into The Devil's Hole, snorting beads of blood until my body floated on the suface like a coat.

Throughout those hopeless months, Master Larkin was my father, my mother, my Mary Margaret. And then, on the day I left his school forever, he betrayed me too.

We were in the parlour, immured from the world by his beloved books. I was in his arms, weeping for the horror of my life.

His voice changed and he cursed the whispers in The Widow Tynan's. The complaints about his teaching. The time lost on useless information. His disappearance every weekend. The nudges, winks, rumours.

When he mentioned a vacancy in some southern town, I didn't need to hear another word. I tore myself away and started grabbing at his shelves. He just stood there as *De Bello Gallico*, *Metamorphoses*, the complete works of Virgil flew around his head, crashed against the wall like birds against the window-pane. Even when, one after the other, his treasured six-volume Gibbon exploded from my hands, he didn't move an inch. Just stood there, impassive as a martyr gazing at the mounting pyre of books.

When every single book lay broken at his feet, I screamed 'I never loved you anyway.'

Next morning there was a knock on our door. My uncle answered it and I heard him giving directions. Pretending that I needed light to read, I sat for hours by the window until, at last, the dray trundled up the road. Shuffling along behind it, Master Larkin stared at his mutilated library as if it was his mother's coffin. I never saw him again.

The town mocked my suffering. It caused my parents years of pain and killed them in the end. The town sent Mary Margaret home to die. It took Master Larkin from me. It crucified me for The Rule of Love. And never once did I cry for vengeance.

At fifteen years of age, Louis Braille gave reading to the blind. Mozart wrote his fourteenth symphony; Verdi his first. Charles I was seduced by his governess. Nietzsche flogged a nymphomaniac with a riding whip. The Mad Maneen was two feet short of normal height. The Alchemist of Love was utterly alone.

The Widow Tynan was picking raspberries when she found my Mary Margaret. Floating like Ophelia in The Devil's Hole. Her breast a jagged honeycomb of blood. And, beside her, Loney's head hanging from a hinge of fur.

Here's another story:
    One hot summer's day, while he was slaving in the haggard, 'Rock Island Line' burst from the kitchen window and changed Murt McCormack's life forever. For two minutes thirty-seven seconds, he stood rooted to the ground, oblivi-

ous to the horseflies and his father's puzzled insults. When the music stopped, he threw away his pitchfork and ran into the house. He emptied the biscuit tin hidden in the wardrobe, stole a handful of change from his father's Sunday suit, and drove the tractor into town to buy his first guitar. He was a month short of his sixteenth birthday.

In JOE'S ELECTRICAL SUPPLIES, he grabbed the only model on display — one-eighth plywood sprayed a dazzling sunburst finish — and dropped the money on the counter. Joe's wife threw in a plectrum, a cord with tasselled ends, and a faded *Play a Tune a Day*.

It took three weeks to tune the strings and figure out E minor. Three weeks of food gone cold outside the bedroom door, his mother crying in the kitchen, his father cursing her for rearing such a gobshite. Another week and another finger changed E minor to E major. Six months later, his fingertips like leather, he could play twenty-seven chords and grin like Lonnie Donegan.

A year after his conversion in the haggard, his father ordered him to 'Drop that bloody yoke or lave the house for good'. He borrowed his mother's egg money, kissed the tears from her cheeks, and wrapped the guitar in a Mackey's seed sack. Crossing the yard, he waved to his father who, in reply, threatened him with a sprong.

Murt was smart enough to know that Murt McCormack would never appear in lights. Somewhere between thinking of his mother and tapping out the rhythm of the wheels, it came to him. When the train pulled into the city, Marty Field stepped off to change the world.

After weeks of hunger in a basement flat, so cold his fingers refused to find a single note, he spotted a postcard in a window and, next day, The Rock Island Linesmen started to rehearse. They dreamed of cappucinos and what they would wear on '6.5 Special'. They warned each other not to 'Rock me daddy-o', and copied every song by Lonnie Donegan. By the time The Linesmen felt ready for their first performance, the skiffle craze was over.

No-one knows what happened to the others but, following stints as dishwasher, deliveryman and, finally, a winter bent beneath a sandwich board for ALFIE'S ALLNIGHT COAL, Marty polished his guitar and joined a showband.

Of course I'm serious. Didn't I tell you every word's the truth?

These were the best years of his life. Money in his pocket, silver suits, nocturnal fish and chips. Crowded vans, black with dust from Danceland, Dreamland, Roseland, speeding through quiet midland towns. Three years of feeling country girls behind windswept parish halls. Three years laughing at the same joke:

Why is Ballypickas like a pair of drainpipes?

Because it has no ballroom.

When the van door crushed his fingers, Marty Field changed his name to Murt McCormack and, overnight, became a manager. One of his protégés, a blind girl tied by polio to a wheelchair, nearly had a hit with 'Walking Back to Happiness', but after grooming half-a-dozen failures, driving six hundred and ninety-seven thousand miles, it dawned on him there must be better ways to make a shilling.

Policemen, sightseers and reporters questioned us for weeks. The Devil's Hole was roped off and the village watched like cattle as frogmen slithered in and out. Diggers unearthed bowls of butter, medieval shoes, a leather jerkin, antlers of every shape and size, a young man's head with perfect auburn hair.

What?

Organic materials can survive for centuries in the anaerobic conditions of the bog.

What?

Lack of oxygen. Did you go to school at all?

They took away the head and spread the rest on a moneen like the innards of some prehistoric beast. Every day brought something new; something to be oohed and aahed at in museums, but not a sign of the weapon that murdered Mary Margaret.

One of the reporters got wind of my cousin's artistry with knives and, day and night, he skulked around the village, waiting to pounce on any word he could twist to fill a page. It was only when Uncle Joe swore he'd gut him with a slane that he finally drove away, muttering about 'those savages still allowed to roam the wilds'.

They did, in fact, take John to the barracks, but let him home the same night.

What?

The thought did cross my mind, but, for all his talk of blood and guts, I knew he wouldn't harm a fly.

What frog?

That was years ago. He was only a child.

And then, as if she had never shared the same air, the same sunlight, the same fear of pain, the world abandoned Mary Margaret. What's a bogman's daughter? What's someone else's child and Christmas just around the corner?

I still cried myself to sleep. The villagers still put flowers on her grave, but, to the world, she might never have existed.

She was everywhere and nowhere.

Everyone I spoke to had her face, yet my dreaming hands clutched only waves of creosote. I heard her laughter singing in my ears. I saw her mouth stuffed with clay. The language we once shared — *adimba, bdimba, cdimba* — was sometimes honey, sometimes ashes on my tongue. Her dress was radiant in the darkness. It was a habit slimy from the grave.

Today, butterflies were emblems of our love; tomorrow, death's-heads swarming from the cracks of tombs.

Mary Margaret was gone and all I had was the memory of creosote. The tang of creosote on my lips.

What do they think I am? Colourblind? Some sort of moron?

Cesare breezed in this morning and spread out these cards, ten of them, with different coloured inkblots.

'What does this one look like?'

'Does it remind you of anything?'

'What do you see here?'

I told him he should use a biro.

Death drove me to the furthest depths of alchemy. I spent nights fingering ancient texts, my eyes bloodshot by the words of thrice-blessed Hermes. *Megistos! Megistos! Megistos!* In *Physica et Mystica*, I learned how, just like man, metals grow and change. As the human soul perfects itself

101

by death and resurrection, so metals aspire to the purity of gold. Black. White. Yellow. I studied the correspondence between macrocosm and microcosm. As above, so below. In *The Book of Lamsprinck*, I found the salamander, born of fire and thriving in its flames. From Paracelsus, I learned how metallic medicines could cure every known disease. The Elixir of Life. The magic of Our Lady's Mantle. Agrippa, Boehme, Geber. I was familiar with them all. I understood fifteen hundred years of alchemy and what was my conclusion? A sham, a complete waste of time and effort. There is no alchemy but The Alchemy of Love. No magic, no miraculous transmutation but the simple alchemy of hands.

Triumphant in the flames of hatred, I am The Salamander of Love. I am the thrice-blessed Alchemist of Love. *Megistos! Megistos! Megistos!*

What kept me going at all? Kept me groping through a wilderness of days; nights that fell like fever.

I'll tell you what. The Rule of Love and my Uncle Joe.

I cured every ailment known to Tonelemona, even those whose mystery struck terror in my neighbours' hearts. I drove grog-blossom from The Zulu's cheeks. In The Widow Tynan I diagnosed anuria and, next morning, she was pissing like a horse. I rid the village of chilblains, thrush, cradlecap, worms and halitosis. I cured Mary Margaret's sister of Saint Vitus's Dance; Tom Fitzpatrick's ear when he winked at Joe Delaney's wife. On the night before her wedding, I cured Mary Cronin's hirsuties and, a week later, her husband's paraphimosis. Wildfire, Hammertoe, Witch's Milk; my hands cured them all. Athlete's Foot, Peggy's Leg,

Housemaid's Knee, Fiddler's Neck. I could go on and on forever . . . .

According to my uncle, there was nothing, not even the blackest grief, that hard work could not cure. And so, from early May to the end of August, he had me on the bog. And never once did I complain. In fact, I lost myself in work. *Laborare est orare*, and every tired muscle, every bead of sweat, was a prayer for Mary Margaret. From dawn until foxes barked at twilight, I stopped only to refresh myself with watercress and handfuls of the streams that web the bog like crystal veins.

In the beginning, Joe would only let me use the flatcher. But when he saw how cleanly I could scrape the 'fum', he said that maybe I could chance my father's slane. I had never handled it before but, within a week, they were standing back in admiration.

The four parts became my incantation to the gift of strength:

> Blade, spade-tree, shaft, hilt.
> Dig, loosen, lift, throw.
> Blade, spade-tree, shaft, hilt.
> Dig, loosen, lift, throw . . . .

When the time came to foot the turf, my *coirceoga* could withstand a hurricane, and, when I built the gable-rick, you would swear it was designed by an architect.

In wintertime, I hunted eels, and, afterwards, sat for hours at the kitchen table, cleaning my father's spear until it shone like silver. Late at night, when John wasn't there to moider me with women, I read the books I ordered through *The Midland Star*. I never thought of Master Larkin.

What?

Of course they did. Annie was forever at me: 'Them that has the brains should use them. Think how proud you'd make your poor Mammy.'

But, I ask you, what need had I of five years in a class of jeering townies? Scholars! Still making faces at sentences I could recite when I was six.

By the time I was seventeen, I had read two thousand, nine hundred and forty-seven books, and, from every single one, I learned something more about the sadness of this world.

I recognise the boots, the navy laces, the dubbin I brought him from The Widow Tynan's. My gaze ascends the moleskins, the lemon stain between the legs, the blackened leather belt.

The calloused hands are held in supplication. From one hangs a young tree, its branches dripping blood, and, draped across the other, a white dress hacked to ribbons.

I turn my eyes from the star on his forehead, but I can't escape the words braying from the monstrous yellow teeth.

'Did I, Equus Asinus Purtock, not endure the furnaces of Africa; centuries of sand and scorching air? And still you had no pity: your whingeing was a trying-iron through my heart. Did I not stumble through the Pillars of Hercules, tamed by stones and Spanish whips? I suffered this for you. And how did you thank me? You dragged your poor mother like a corpse through the town.

'At Hastings, Agincourt, Ramillies, Austerlitz, did I not die a million deaths? And lived to die again with shame at what I'd brought into this world. A maneen. A runt. The

Alchemist of Love!

'Was I not beaten onto ships, screaming for sickness to quell my churning pain? Was I not lashed into a wilderness of bogs and endless rain? And, for this, you made me a buffoon; the laughing-stock of those who, for generations, revered the Purtocks' mastery of the slane. Your whingeing did this to me. And your poor mother too. Your whingeing broke her heart and drove her to an early grave. And the words you threw at me, brandished in my face with the arrogance of flags. Should I be punished for my lack of words?'

Blood is flowing from his ruined eyes.

'And you think you have reason to complain! You can't sleep. You can't trust the food. No-one loves you. No-one will listen to the truth. . . .'

He has asked me half-a-dozen times and I always found some excuse. But he and Annie have been so good to me, I can't refuse forever. I should have known better.

Picture this:

It is Michaelmas Eve and, for the second time in my life, I am on my way to town. Perched on top of the load, Uncle Joe is playing his bird game. 'Try this,' he says, then whistles a few notes, and waits for me to identify the bird. I know them all at once but, to please him, I frown and tap a finger to my lips. Pride makes his plain face lovable and he asks me to try again.

He trills 'If I were a blackbird' and his mouth is like my mother's when she wanted me to kiss her. I remember all the times I tried to squirm away, and a lump gathers in my throat. I see her stretched on my father's grave, her dying hands tearing at the myrtle bush. To drive away the memory, I throw back my head and copy Joe: 'If I were a blackbird, I'd whistle and sing . . . .'

We pass the crumbling factory; the bridge where my father cursed the train; the office of the lawyer whose name is flung at me today. The Square is still empty as I steer past the Virgin with her halo of electric bulbs; the horse trough and, broken only by a butcher's and JOE'S ELECTRICAL SUPPLIES, a row of seven public houses. Joe warns me to watch my head and we turn through the archway into Fagan's yard.

We have the turf unloaded in no time and I follow him into a passageway rank with piss and disinfectant.

Two hours and six pints later, Joe finally agrees it's 'time to look for Annie's bird'.

What?

I did not. All my life I have had no truck with alcohol. Have you been brainwashed too? The drunken nights in The House of Love. Women falling into the streets at dawn. Do you believe everything you hear? Do you listen to every monstrous whisper? All my life, nothing ever passed my lips but milk and water. My body was blessed with The Alchemy of Love. Do you think I would profane it with filth of any kind? You only have to look around you. . . . Even that mob outside my window, for all their show of piety, can't disguise the mottled faces, the sunken eyes. Spines twisted from the beast with two backs. Listen to them. Their wheezy voices damning me with hymns. *In vino ignominia*. Even Lucrezia. The other morning, she had these bruises on her neck. Teethmarks. And she dares question me!

'Did you love your mother?'

'Did you love your father?'

'Was your little friend precocious for her age?'

Animals. Dogs in the street the lot of them.

Where was I? Yes. Over by the Market Wall, the Goose Fair has begun. Townspeople, farmers, children peer into carts and trailers; circle clumps of huddled birds. From the doorway of a yellow caravan, a tinker girl is bawling 'Nell Flaherty's Drake'. There are geese in pens; tied in sacks; craning from the boots of cars. Here and there, Joe stops to haggle over weights and prices and, when he finally settles for a small plump Roman, I have to force myself not to think of Master Larkin. No. That's not true. He never even crossed my mind. When the deal is struck, the palms spat on, we thread our way back to the yard.

On the way home, we pass a crowd of young lads outside a chip-shop. One of them shouts 'Squirt!' and flicks a cigarette butt into the cart. Joe waves his fist, but that only makes them worse. The street erupts in laughter — 'Squirt!' 'Shorty!' 'Maneen!' — and, as Joe goads the donkey forward, I stand defiant as a prisoner in the tumbril.

But I bore no malice towards the town. Even when it persecuted me a third time . . . .

You would think John was getting married. First he squashed into the tin bath and got me to scrub his back. He even made me dig dried blood from underneath his nails. Then he stood for ages at the mirror, grimacing as his father's cut-throat drew loving arcs across his face. I envied him and searched my chin in vain for any sign of roughness.

Next, he doused his head in a basin until his wavy hair was straight, splashed himself with lavender water, put on what he called 'the townie togs', and finally, twisted his tie into a perfect windsor.

Throughout this ritual, I observed him from an armchair, wondering how I had ever let him talk me into going. But if you can't oblige your own flesh and blood, what's the point in anything?

Picture this:

Danceland is packed for the Tenth Annual Victuallers' Ball. Condensation trickles down the walls. The floor undulates like rubber. And there am I, The Alchemist of Love, the arms pulled off me by my cousin and some drunken butcher in a waistcoat. Round and round we go in a frantic Paul Jones. Round and round, crazed peasants whirling round the Maypole. Why am I doing this? Why am I here at all? Every few seconds, the butcher slaps his hair back on his naked head and the circle threatens to explode. I see myself careering towards the wall, but, just in time, he grabs my hand, winks as if I was a woman, and round and round we go again.

The shirt is stuck to my back; my feet are on fire, but there is no escape. Round and round and round in a blur of clothes and faces. Suddenly we stop and, when the hall rights itself, a girl about my own age is smiling from the lacquered helmet of her hair. I have to drag my eyes from her cleavage. Even in advertisements, I have never seen a dress cut so low.

John calls my name and appears beside me with a woman old enough to be his mother.

'Say hello to the ladies . . . .'

'Pussy got your tongue?' the girl laughs, and I feel like hitting her; slapping her so hard that the shiny helmet will roll across the floor. But I just stand there, my face burning, knitting my fingers like a fool.

John whispers something in her ear and, before I know it, we are squirming through the crowd, the woman glued to his side, me pulled along by her friend's clammy hand. I haven't uttered a single word, and here I am, following her like a lost child. All I have to do is pull away my hand and disappear through the walls of sweaty clothes; hide for a while, then go home and wait for John. Why is he doing this to me? Him of all people. He knows of my devotion to Mary Margaret; my vow never to even look at anyone else. The Rule of Love never needed any carnal satisfaction.

Five or six townies are lounging at the door. They throw friendly insults at the girls and joke about 'the butcher and his little shop-boy'. John warns me to ignore them and leads us into darkness behind the hall. The music sounds strange; all a muffled thud of drums, and it's a minute before I recognise 'A Mother's Love's a Blessing'.

John and the woman fall onto the grass and a thrill of fear runs along my spine. The girl squeezes my hand. Her fingertips are on my cheek. Just like Mary Margaret when she licked the sweat from my dreaming eyes. I am disgusted with myself. How could I defile our love by thinking of it now? This stranger is pressing herself against me, peppermint breath whispering her name is Bernie. Something is happening to my body and I grope for something to repel it.

Mensa, mensa, mensam, mensae, mensae, mensa.

Footsteps crunch the gravel and she jerks away, pointing to the ground. As they drag John off the sprawled woman, she fixes her clothes and laughs: 'Jesus lads, ye took yeer time. The bastard has me et.'

There must be nine or ten or them, prodding us with fists, spattering our clothes with spit.

'Bogmen, fucking bogmen,' they sneer, and their laughter chills me to the bone.

'A mother's love's a blessing . . . .'

'Bitch', John hisses, and a knife flashes in his hand. A boot sends it ringing against the wall. A second kick gets him right between the legs and he falls to his knees, squealing like a stuck pig.

'Fucking bogmen. Trying our women!'

A fist crashes into his jaw and he topples backwards, groaning at my feet.

'Your mother always loved you . . . .'

Another kick and he is puking. They go to lift him, but he crumples to the ground.

I am alone. The Alchemist of Love is utterly alone. At the mercy of the town that hated him from birth. I close my eyes against the boot, the fist that will bring crimson stars of pain, but no; they just crowd around me, so close I can smell their eager sweat.

'Dirty fucking bogman!'

'Trying our women!'

'He'd need a fucking ladder!'

'The butcher might put him up to it!'

'Miracle fucking Mickey!'

How do they know who I am? Has the magic of my hands infiltrated pubs and dancehalls?

Then I realise it is John who has filled the town with tales of his miraculous cousin, and, for an instant, I don't care if he never walks again.

'Dirty fucking bogman!' and suddenly their paws are on me.

'There's no-one like your mother . . . .'

But no, they don't pummel me to the ground or send me reeling through the dark.

'Give us a look at Miracle Mickey,' the girl guffaws, and my coat is torn from me.

'The Mad Maneen!' and my shirt is ripped to tatters.

'Dirty fucking bogman!' and I am on the ground, flailing at their arms.

They pull off my trousers and jump back into another

circle. Can you see the picture? The Alchemist of Love is stripped of his garments, scourged by the hatred flying from their tongues.

'Give us that yoke, Bernie!' and suddenly my face is drenched in sweetness; anointed with stinging drops of perfume. My nakedness is smeared with the smell that lured me from the hall. A spray hisses between my legs and makes a desperate fig leaf of my hands.

'Miracle Mickey. Wash yourself before you come to town!'

'You'll never miss your dear old Mam till she's buried beneath the clay.'

And then they are gone. Vanished into darkness; their laughter hanging in the scented air. On my hands and knees, weeping aromatic tears, I fumble for my clothes.

'Everyone. All together now. One last time. A mother's love's a blessing . . . .'

The world begins to fade, to slip away as if I am waking from a dream, and a cold sweat envelops me until all I see is Mary Margaret's mutilated breast.

What have I done to deserve such humiliation? All my life I observed the sacred Rule of Love and this is how they thank me. But I bear no malice, no desire for revenge. I pity those poor fools: their gleaming hair; crashing fists; the anger fuming from their lips. I pity their meagre lives. Their dependence on this town. Better a dinner of herbs where love is than a stalled ox and hatred therewith.

A week after I cured Auntie Annie's emphysema, *The Midland Star* proclaimed WOMAN'S MIRACLE CURE. Next morning, a van pulled up outside the gate and a stranger banged the door. When I told him yes, I was Mister Purtock, his withered fingers offered me a card edged with silver stars. MARTIN McCORMACK. INTERNATIONAL AGENT AND IMPRESARIO.

At eighteen years of age, Victoria was Queen of England; Frederick the Great watched his best friend being beheaded, and Hedy Lamarr appeared absolutely naked in 'Extase'. The Emperor Elabolus was murdered by the Praetorian Guard; his body, painted, perfumed and dressed in women's clothes, dragged on hooks through the city he once had scandalised. Tutankhamen died at eighteen, and, to give the world The Rule of Love, I left Tonelemona.

He put an advertisement in a shop window and rented out the back room of a pub in Kilburn. That first evening, under posters of hurling teams, trains snaking through nostalgic fields, two people found the magic of my hands. A woman crippled with arthritis. A man who held my hand and whispered he was dying twice: of loneliness for the village he abandoned; of shame at seeing his children grow up foreigners.

In the beginning, they were mostly immigrants. Youths worn out by building sites and beer, coldwater flats, weeks sleeping in their clothes. Old men who had never lost their accents. Always going home next year.

I soon discovered why. Behind my back, Murt had handed out a thousand posters of a bishop in garish emerald robes. THE PATRON SAINT OF HEALING was printed in a halo and, all around him, bathed in celestial light, HOMESICKNESS? PROBLEMS WITH THE DRINK? ANY ILLNESS, PHYSICAL, MENTAL,

I nearly killed him. Only his shrieks of how hard it was to live with one good hand stopped me from tearing him apart. I eventually controlled my rage and, in a fit of remorse, cured his twisted fingers. But not before I had warned him that never, never again, no matter how the world conspired against me, should The Rule of Love be defiled in such a way. I had no need of any meretricious schemes. I knew the gospel would be spread by all who knelt before me. And I was right. A month later, we had to call a policeman to stop them breaking down the door.

I had never dreamed there could be so much misery, so much suffering. A whole universe of pain converged on one tiny room; men and women of every creed and colour pleading for the miracle their prayers had sought in vain; children unaware of how this world had blighted them forever.

Naked came ye from your mother's womb. Naked shall ye be healed. Some demurred at first and challenged me with their eyes; others turned and stormed away. But none was ever denied The Alchemy of Love. Young, old, the cynical and the desperate; my hands cured them all. The aquatic limbs of infants. Rancid blubber. Skin that rustled at my touch.

What?

Why should I? After everything they did to me? Is a prophet not without honour, save in his own country? A what? Are you serious? Have I ever claimed to be a patriot? I spit on those who die for any cause but love. I spit on *dulce et decorum est*.

Will you stop interrupting me? Do you want the truth or not?

In a swirl of blood, the *dullahán* gallops back and forth across my eyes. Streaming from the spear in his side, the white dress is a shrill triumphant flag.

I spent years racing up and down motorways that never seemed to change, every mile accompanied by yet another song by Lonnie Donegan. For a man with no voice, Murt never tired of singing. I used to fall asleep and, hours later, he was still at it, grinning at his teeth in the windscreen, his new fingers tapping out contentment on the wheel. But I didn't mind. I always loved music. At least until they brought me here. Do you know what they had today? One of those gramophones with the big horns. I laughed when this old woman trundled along the avenue and cranked it up outside my window. It's a wonder she didn't bring the dog. All morning, until the porter threatened to call the police, 'Panis Angelicus' crackled from John McCormack's throat. I wonder is he any relation of Murt's?

I never demanded payment for the magic of my hands. But you must be realistic. Man does not live by bread alone. There were clothes, petrol, hotel bills, to be thought of. Anyway, is not the labourer worthy of his hire?

I was spending more money than Tonelemona ever knew existed. Notes pressed into my fist, envelopes left behind on chairs. Cheques that, only for Murt, might never have been cashed. He took twenty-five per cent and every other penny was posted home to Uncle Joe. Who deserved it more? I also sent something every month to Mrs Dunne. It was the least I could do. Had she not given me her daughter? I arranged for a firm in the city to erect a memorial — a plain marble stone inscribed *adimba, bdimba, cdimba* — over Mary Margaret's grave. It wasn't until years later that The Widow Tynan told me how I was rewarded. The minute the workmen drove away, Paddy Dunne and half the village, shaking with biblical rage, smashed it into pieces.

Even my own people turned against me.

Where was I?

Why am I so easily distracted? My mind just seems to float away. Are they at my food again? Or maybe it's the water? That must be it. They have drugs to kill the truth; every sort of poison to make you more like them. In future I'll demand that Cesare sips it first.

And it wasn't just money. They embarrassed me with gifts I had no use for: bits of jewellery, free tickets, pots of jam, homemade cakes and bread. Some even offered me their bodies. Every night, for six or seven years, I could have had more sex than Solomon. At first, I was shocked by the phone numbers, the invitations thrust into my hand, whispered in my ear. But were they not just a token of their gratitude, of how deeply I had changed their lives? A lesser man would certainly have succumbed, but The Alchemist of Love wanted nothing in return. He was doing no more than he was made for.

All those years, I never spent a penny on myself. The Rule of Love is not ambitious; it seeketh not its own. No, that's not quite true. Everywhere I went I bought books, thousands of books, and sent them home to be stored in my parents' cottage. I always knew that some day I would return to Tonelemona.

And, of course, I bought the Silver Shadow.

Picture this:

We are in the furthest north of Scotland, driving through the most wondrous storm I have ever seen. One minute, perfect sheets of darkness skewered on the headlights; the next, a blinding shock of white. The rain attacks the van like darts and, for once, Murt is not Lonnie Donegan, but a hunchback on the wheel, staring into something terrible.

Did I tell you that I have always venerated storms? As a child I used to stand at the window, dumbstuck by the *son et lumière* in the yard. But, most of all, I love how a storm scatters the high and mighty of this world. I love how they run like mice from its fiery claws, the thunder of their arrogance stolen by the sky. And wasn't it a storm that delivered my precious piece of glass, and a storm that finally brought her back to me?

I am thinking of Julia Purtock when, suddenly, the van splutters to a halt.

What?

I'll tell you later.

Cursing the heavens, Murt tries the engine and bangs the dashboard with his fist. Another flash makes terror of his anger and he cowers in the seat, his head hidden in his hands. Calmly I open the map. We are no more than a mile or two from the town. When I suggest that we get out and walk, he jerks alive and, muttering prayers I haven't heard since Mary Margaret's funeral, grabs a torch and disappears outside. I can hear him mumbling as the bonnet looms before me. Half-a-dozen times, he comes and goes, stamping on pedals, prodding the ignition, his hair in rats' tails on his forehead.

Why didn't I help him? I'll tell you why. The most valuable trait a man can possess is the ability to recognise when he is useless. Utterly impotent in any situation. I am the epitome of this. I could bang my head against these walls, scream until my throat was dry, strangle Cesare and Lucrezia and vanish just like that. But what's the point? I know it's only a matter of time before I am vindicated and return in glory to The House of Love. That's all, just a matter of time.

When I tell him it's only a short walk into town, he glances at me as if I was a slow child; something to be humoured. Then he wants to wait until the storm dies down. Did you ever hear such nonsense? I had people waiting for me; people whose happiness depended on me. All my life I had never disappointed anyone.

Can you see the picture?

The Alchemist of Love strides into darkness and, splashing along behind, cursing every rumble, every drop of rain, his international agent and impresario.

Next morning, he persuaded me to 'lave that other yoke for the tinkers and buy a real machine'. I left the choice to him — what did I know about cars? I could barely drive — and so, a few days later, he pulled up outside the hotel in a gleaming Silver Shadow.

To me, it was just another way of getting us from A to B, but I was amazed at the effect it had on others. They stood in the street to ogle us; policemen smiled; children ran along behind us. When they dragged me from The House of Love, they kicked and taunted it with sticks. You'd think it was a stubborn donkey. Imagine getting angry with a car.

Murt treated it with a respect that made me shudder. He spent hours just sitting in it; whole days washing it and chatting to his reflection. He even gave up smoking, and woe betide the smallest insect that blundered through a window. And that was just the start. I came down one morning and there he was, in a puce suit and pillbox hat, bowing

117

beside the open door. I soon put a stop to his gallop. Who did he think I was? Cinderella?

I'll never forget the row when I tried to hang the Blessed Turf from the mirror. Did I tell you about the Blessed Turf?

On the first day of September, we all brought a sod of turf to the moneen. There it was touched by the youngest child in the village. Blessed by the innocence of a tiny hand. It was then impaled on eel-spears, set on fire, and carried in procession from house to house to ward off disease. Small pieces were sewn into clothes or made into scapulars. Everywhere I went, I had my blessed piece of turf — not because I believed in its talismanic powers, but because I revered it as a symbol. No, much more than a symbol. It was the very rock on which our village was founded. Turf, blessed turf: *erat in principio, et nunc, et semper, et in saecula saeculorum.*

Cesare has just told me that they have decided on a day. I must hurry if I am to finish this chronicle of truth. But no, why should I accommodate them? Why should I be meek; let them load me into a van and parade me through streets already poisoned by their lies? They took me from The House of Love. They will not succeed a second time. I have a plan.

Sometimes I think he must have been stone mad. Do you know what he wanted me to do? Hire out the Royal Albert Hall. Did you ever hear the likes? What did he think I was?

A crooner in a monkey suit? How could my hands reach such a multitude? Do you think I would abuse my gift like that? Of course I could have filled anywhere I wanted, but I needed intimacy. Closeness. Propinquity. I needed to feel my love penetrate the skin. And so I travelled every byroad in the country, often so exhausted I couldn't even sleep. I used to stay awake for days, then collapse into a coma. Murt used to fly into a terrible panic. After all, wasn't I his golden goose? I am not naive. I know my own worth. If it wasn't for me, he would still be peddling stardust.

I remember, once, I fell into a heap on the pavement, and when I came to, there was a wall of white coats around the bed. I screamed at those Hippocratic fools — were they any better than the bastards that ran my father from the hotel, or pawed Mary Margaret? — and warned Murt if they were ever let within an ass's roar of me again, he could say goodbye to his twenty-five per cent. There was nothing wrong with me. I was never a day sick in all my life. All I needed was sleep. The second most important thing in life: dreamless uninvaded sleep.

I was a celebrity; stopped in the street, invited to the most exclusive parties, argued over in the press. One rag wondered if they were witnessing The Second Coming. Another warned the nation of the Antichrist. A prouder man would have revelled in such nonsense. The Messiah! I am The Alchemist of Love. No more, no less. Just The Alchemist of Love.

What?

Of course you didn't. How could you? From the very beginning, there was a conspiracy against me. Do you think they would be interested in me — a bogman, a jumped-up peasant from the Midlands? Look how quickly they dropped Mary Margaret.

Did John Larkin murder Mary Margaret?

No, I am deadly serious. Consider the following:

(a) His background. Was it not what you might call 'shady'? No-one had any idea where he came from. What's this the priest said? The county beyond the mountains. There are seventeen counties beyond the mountains.

(b) He taught in twenty different schools. Wanderlust, he called it, but that was only half the truth. Did he violate others there as well? When he rode into our village that first August evening, did he leave a trail of blood behind him?

(c) Where did he disappear to every single weekend? Answer me that. Was he searching for another victim?

(d) He never liked Mary Margaret because she distracted me from him. Is that not motive enough?

(e) I saw the eel-spear in his kitchen.

(f) Why did he run away straight after her death? There can only be one answer.

I have presented my evidence to Cesare and Lucrezia, and it won't be long before a warrant is issued for his arrest. Wherever he is lurking, they will find him, and Mary Margaret will finally rest in peace.

Sundew, Rosemary, Butterwort, Ling.
Crowberry, Juniper, Bilberry, Birch.
Curlew, Skygoat, Kestrel, Grouse.
Frog, Hare, Otter, Eel.

The names were a lullaby; a litany of remembrance. No matter where I was, all I had to do was say the words and I was home again. I didn't even have to close my eyes. And, all the time, weaving through my tired head, the songs my mother used to sing. 'The Old Bog Road', 'The Sky O'er Tonelemona', 'The Cutter and his Lass'. Is there anything more moving? You're welcome to the intricacies of Bach, Mozart's way with melody, Wagner's *Sturm und Drang*. Nothing melts the heart like a sentimental song.

For all our disagreements, I have to admit that Murt McCormack knew his business, and, so, one after the other, the five continents bowed before me. For ten more years, through ice and snow, searing wind and heat, I followed my vocation. I won't bore you with the suffering and wonders I encountered. Neither will I boast of my success. Suffice to say that my hands touched anyone who needed them and, despite my indifference to all worldly goods, I found myself a very wealthy man.

But there was something missing. There was an emptiness that all the gold of Croesus could not fill. And then, one night, somewhere in Venezuela, it came to me. The Alchemist of Love was homesick. The rhymes, my mother's

121

songs, my anger when Murt did something wrong, were all just signs of discontent. I remember exactly how it happened. Murt was outside shooing a gang of urchins from the car. As I lay in bed, exhausted by the thousands who had sought my hands, I began to hear voices. At first, I thought they were coming from the next room. Then I thought my schedule had finally taken its toll and I was having some sort of breakdown. The room was a small box bursting with a multitude of voices. Voices I recognised. Like Saint Patrick, I was being called on to return. They were beseeching me to come home and heal them with my love.

That very night, I made a millionaire of Murt, threw my arms around his neck and said goodbye to him forever.

They say he was once a mammoth wandering prehistoric plains; a wolf trapped in medieval minds; an eagle snatching deadmen's eyes. He can assume any shape he wants and, for longer than the memory of blood, he has stalked the dreams of children. On the night of Michaelmas, his stink drives them from every fruit tree in the country. The cheesy fungus that is his emblem causes instant death. But his chief delight is to lure them on his stallion's back and vanish like the wind.

He is smiling and patient. He can kill with words that make you love him. You will forget your own family; abandon any notion of what is right or wrong. For the pleasure of his body, you will crawl across your mother's corpse.

He may wear a suit and dazzle you with oxblood boots.

This is how the *pooka* murdered Mary Margaret.

Listen to that bawling. SEVENTEEN! SEVENTEEN! Even little children. PURTOCK IS A MONSTER. HOLY GOD WILL GET THE EVIL BOGMAN.

So horrified was he to discover that, unlike marble statues, women sprouted pubic hair, John Ruskin was unable to consummate his marriage. He was thirty-five when his young wife finally left him. At the same age, Nelson lost an eye, Flaubert published *Madame Bovary*, and Cortez brought terror to the Aztecs. Saint Bernadette, Crazy Horse, Mozart, all died at thirty-five. After half his life spent healing half the world, The Mad Maneen returned to Tonelemona.

My father used to boast that, even on a wet night, 'the blindest city gent couldn't help but see the bonfire'. I don't know about that, but, with ten miles still to go, the red patch in the sky told me I was home.

For centuries, the village has celebrated Saint John's Eve with a festival of light. Trailing manes of flame, children run from house to house with torches; fires burn in every yard and, at midnight, everyone gathers on the moneen, singing and dancing until the bonfire is just a heap of embers.

Next evening, the ash is sprinkled on the gardens. Did you know that Tonelemona once produced the finest vegetables in the country? Cabbages as big as pumpkins, carrots thicker than your arm. And then, in yet another scheme to kill the boglands, someone started growing them under glass. Acres and acres of artificial sun designed to keep the bogman in the dark. Did you know that? Of course you didn't. You only hear about us when some poor fool is barred from The Widow Tynan's, and wanders into town begging for a drink. *The Midland Star* will tell you that alright. DRUNK AND DISORDERLY. DISTURBING THE PEACE. Look at it today: six-inch letters screaming THIS ANIMAL MUST BE CAGED!

What are they going to do when I am free? When The Rule of Love is once again triumphant? Persecute The Zulu until he buys a licence for the jackass? The Widow Tynan for selling us poteen?

Contrary to popular belief, reporters are not failed or would-be writers. They are failed human beings. Hollow men held together by the thrill of seeing their by-line over someone else's pain. I'm telling you, they can hardly spell their names, never mind make any kind of sense. NOMADIC DWELLERS OF THE LIBYAN DESSERT. GRAND OLD MAN OF FRENCH LETTERS DIES IN RIDING ACCIDENT. LOCAL CHILD HIT BY TRAIN RUSHED TO TWO HOSPITALS. I'm serious. I saw them myself. And the same upstarts dare impugn the sacred Rule of Love.

Anyway, there I was, my eyes blurred with tears, trying to keep the Silver Shadow in the middle of the lane. Those were the longest ten miles I have ever travelled and, when the headlights finally found my mother's elders, I had to stop, I was so exhausted by emotion. The Alchemist of Love was home.

The village was deserted, but I could hear music drifting from the moneen. I stood at the gate and closed my eyes, trembling in the grip of memory. My father's pipesmoke coiling in the summer air. The form where Mary Margaret sat astonished by my every word. My terror in the tool shed. The rick that vanished up the chimney. Her laughter; her tongue flicking at my cheek; her mouth nuzzling towards her mother's breast. The tang of creosote on our lips. Her eyes reflecting silver stars.

The silence made me turn. The moneen was still a pyramid of flame, but there wasn't the slightest sound of revelry. In the blink of an eye, or so it seemed, the bog had opened, snatched the dancers' heels and closed on them again.

I have never felt such calm. I could hear sweat trickling from my forehead; wisps of bog cotton sailing to the ground.

Then I heard footsteps. My fist tightened on the gate as a spectral procession, a cortege of shadows, approached along the lane. The elders hid them for a moment and, when they reappeared, I could sense the questions in their eyes.

Who's that snooping around the Purtock place?

Remember Paddy Dunne's young one.

Are there others, hiding in the ditches, behind the lights?

Could we not be left alone this holy night?

Maybe it's only tourists, swells from the town led astray by beer?

I strode into the light and before a word could leave my mouth, MIRACLE MICKEY filled the space between us. My cousin. After all the years, I recognised his voice as surely as my own. Can you blame me for bursting into tears?

'It's only Miracle Mickey. The Man Maneen', he roared again, and suddenly the shadows were a mob bruising me in welcome.

'You never told us you were coming!'

'Where did you find the motor?'

'Begob he's hardly gained an inch.'

My uncle pumped my hand and the smell of poteen swept away the years. Annie nearly smothered me; The Widow Tynan wet my face with tears. 'The poor maneen', she whimpered, 'the poor little maneen. I always knew you'd not forget us.'

When John introduced me to his wife and son, I was rooted to the ground. For one delirious instant; a fraction of a second that made a mockery of reason; a thunderclap that scattered time in a million random pieces, nothing ever happened at The Devil's Hole. No screams sent pleasure spurting through a madman's veins. No blood exploded from a young girl's breast. The hands that loved me never clawed at murderous air.

And then the world caught hold of itself again, and I remembered the child who knelt before me, her fingers twitching with Saint Vitus's Dance.

The arm was worn off me, my back slapped a hundred times. Children, whose parents once sniggered at the magic of my tongue, pulled my clothes and danced around me. I was the stranger whose name monopolised their dreams. I was the prodigal son. I was a legend. I was a bogman. I was Miracle Mickey. The Mad Maneen. The Alchemist of Love.

Somehow, I found myself back in the car with youngsters crawling over me. A *bodhrán* started rumbling, and the village marched behind as, down the bog lane, gliding over tussocks, the Silver Shadow purred towards the moneen.

Once, I glanced in the mirror, and the firebrands, the reddened faces, brought vigilantes screaming from The Widow Tynan's Westerns. Was it a premonition; the merest psychic inkling that they would turn against me too? I don't know, but, that night, they honoured my return, not with snuff and tablecloths, but in the way they knew I appreciated most. The continuation of a ritual, a tradition that connected every bogman with the generations gone before him.

I danced with anyone who caught my arm; jigged and reeled until my head was spinning. Young girls, infants when I left; old men whose flashing boots defied the years; mothers I remembered flat-chested as boys. The Widow Tynan grabbed me for a waltz and moidered me with how she had always loved me as her own. Mag Fitzpatrick thanked me half-a-dozen times for ending her humiliation in the cromlech. She stuck her mouth into my ear and shouted how the man above had taken Tom; how young Michael Joseph had to go across the water. How hard it was for a woman on her own. How she'd 'love a jaunt in the motor'.

When our feet could take no more, we sat around the bonfire, unravelling the years, contradicting dates of births, harvests, marriages and deaths.

There was more merriment when the Silver Shadow got stuck in a drain. For half an hour they fell over each other, then gave up and stood around making sagas of every hoof and wheel that ever sank in muck.

When Joe Delaney finally arrived back with the donkeys, it took another hour of laughter to yoke them to the car, and it was dawn before we started off again.

Can you see the picture?

The Mad Maneen seated in his Silver Shadow, rolling home behind a team of grinning donkeys?

ONLY FIFTEEN MORE!

Cesare ambled in this morning and opened out a newspaper. On the front page, a man was peering from a barred window. His hands clutched his cheeks, but you could feel the terror in his eyes.

Where did they get this? What is Cesare up to now? What did I tell you about the press? I will sue that rag for millions; demand an apology in headlines. I know about photography; the lies, the machinations of the darkroom.

Cesare says he knows how hard it is, but I could make it easier by telling him the truth. Jesus Christ, are they minding me at all? Do I have to repeat every word I say? For the very last time, for once and for all, I swear on my mother's grave, by the wounds in Mary Margaret's breast, that every word's the truth.

In the weeks that followed, I must have walked a thousand miles. I left the cottage at first light and didn't turn back till Jack O'Lantern flickered all around me.

I lay on the moneen for hours, describing butterflies to Mary Margaret.

I followed hare runs leading nowhere.

In Joe Lalor's workshop, I caressed the hollow skulls until faces loomed before me, their dead voices ringing in my head.

I strolled around the chapel, my eyes filled with The Lamb of God, the cockfight, my uncle's scissors flashing in the sun.

Kneeling on my parents' grave, I rubbed the myrtle leaves and wept into my scented palms.

Like a pilgrim, I circled Mary Margaret's bones.

I visited the school where the children cheered when Master Hogan asked me back to tell them of my travels. I refused every invitation to his cottage.

I spent nights slumped in lamplight, bored by John's new shop in town; how many beasts he killed each week; how all the women loved him.

Mrs Dunne cried as she showed me Mary Margaret's schoolbooks. The matchstick figures in the margins. Her crooked MM XXX MJ. The butterflies, the self-portrait, a row of smiling dogs I had drawn for her as presents.

She led me into the bedroom and opened the wardrobe I had watched Billy-the-Box making in the yard. The dresses looked so small, so vulnerable. I felt hatred welling in my throat. I wanted to own her clothes. I wanted to lie awake at night enveloped in the memory of her skin.

Over and over again, Paddy asked me how his little girl could be taken and no-one give a damn. He knew what it took me thirty years to learn. There is no justice in this world; no reward for virtue. The meek suffer; the innocent always feel the pain.

In all the time I spent there, they never said a word about her tombstone.

I often fell asleep in my parents' kitchen, and someone found me in the morning, my cheek resting on an open page, the floor strewn with the library I had assembled.

One evening, I watched as Paddy Galvin spancelled the mare and covered her head in a canvas bag. Next, he took a set of fleams from his trousers pocket, inspected them, and chose the smallest blade. For what seemed like ages, he stroked the neck then, suddenly, his hand twitched once and blood spurted in a crimson arc. When it slowed to a trickle, he snapped a hair from the mane, twisted it into an eight and pressed it to the wound.

A week later, The Zulu stormed into our kitchen. First he cursed 'the young crowd who think they know it all', then asked if I would 'throw an eye on the unfortunate baste'.

Next morning, his son was telling everyone how 'the maneen was the bate of any bloody whisperer in the country'.

Another time, a woman I didn't know knocked the door and stood there, gulping back the tears.

'Sit down, Janey, sit down like a good girl,' and my uncle led her to a chair.

It took me a minute to remember the fat girl in Mrs Clancy's; how she used to wobble when my stories made them laugh. She asked if she could have a word with Mister Purtock. Joe sidled into the yard and she started again, her body racked with grief.

Two months ago, she lost a baby and, ever since, wasn't herself at all. Her children were often hungry but she couldn't bear to cook; the sight of meat made her vomit on the table. Three or four nights a week, the villagers found her wandering the bog with her husband's slane.

Suddenly she pulled me towards her and held my head against her womb. Her sobs became a wail and, when Joe appeared in the doorway, my hands were upon her, telling her not to worry any more.

What?

According to tradition, women who miscarried were cursed by the Devil. The foetus was whisked away and buried without a coffin in an unmarked grave.

Yes, I was back among my own people. Every face, every tree and flower, every sod of turf, a reminder of the sanctity of home. Every breath filled with the goodness of the bog, and still I wasn't happy.

The hall is packed, alive with anticipation. Children I knew at school, people I talk to every day, half-forgotten faces, men and women dead for twenty years.

There is a roar when my cousin comes smiling from the wings. He bows to the crowd, his hand unleashes a dart of silver light and the orchestra bursts into 'The Can Can'. The curtain rises and a dog is dancing in a chorus line of naked girls, its hindlegs kicking perfect rhythm to the music, its white dress brilliant in the spotlight. Like handlers at a cockfight, the crowd is baying at the smell of blood . . . .

Among the weeds and bits of rubble, I stood picturing the room. The smell of leather and tobacco, the ordination pictures, souvenirs from Fatima and Lourdes. I heard my father pleading with the priest. I saw the housekeeper listening from the hall. I saw the priest searching for his stole, then calling for a jug of water. Most of all, I heard my own screams.

The same evening, I went to see the priest in his new bungalow. He hummed and hawed for ages — he would have to see the bishop, diocesan committees; he might even have to write to Rome. When I mentioned a figure, he stopped in mid-sentence and assured me he would have everything sorted out within the week.

The villagers throught I was mad. Even worse, some accused me of betrayal.

'What about The Lamb of God?'

'The short shrift your poor father got, even on his deathbed?'

Joe thumped the table and swore that Straightface would

turn in his grave. When I mentioned John's shop, he went purple and looked the other way. Annie sat beside him, snivelling how she had always done her best. Was this how I proposed to thank her? What would people say? Were his own not good enough for him? Imagine how they would sneer in town.

In The Widow Tynan's, they banged glasses on the counter; cursed the maneen for getting too big for his boots.

'All them foreign countries, the money, the big motor, is gone to his head.'

I am not mad. I knew exactly what I wanted. For the first time since Mary Margaret's death, I was happy with my life. And who was I betraying? They had short memories. Thanks to me, Tonelemona was the fittest village in the country.

But who was more in need of love than this accursed town? Who abandoned me at birth and drove my parents to an early grave? Who made no effort to find Mary Margaret's killer? Who nearly blinded me at the Annual Victuallers' Ball. Go on, answer me that.

Love your enemies, do good to them that persecute you. Turn the other cheek. I was doing precisely that.

ONLY TEN MORE!

The fools. Do they really think I will fall into their snares?

Consider this:

Did Joe Lalor fill her head with dreams and lure her to his bed of bones? Did his chisel tear her body open?

Was it her own father? Look what he did to the tombstone. Is it healthy to have so many children under the same roof?

Was she lacerated by my cousin's knife? By The Zulu's atavistic spear?

It took nine months to build The House of Love. Nine months of local industry rubbing its hands with glee; officials in the city marvelling at the sudden drop in unemployment.

From Tonelemona I brought my parents' bed, my father's treasure and his eel-spear, my mother's clock and candles. Everything else, from furniture to bars of soap, I ordered from businesses in town. Didn't I tell you I was the economic saviour of the Midlands?

The House of Love had thirty rooms, each equipped with music and every other comfort. This was not extravagance. People would travel the length and breadth of the country to find the magic of my hands. Should I not at least offer them a bed?

When the library of Alexandria was sacked by the Caliph Omar in 642, it contained enough books to warm the baths of the city for six months. The Lenin State Library in Moscow has twenty million volumes; Harvard University more than eight million. In the year I was born, there were sixty-two books in Tonelemona. In The House of Love, from *Aardvark: Orycteropus Afer. A Study in Morphology*, to *Zyzzophobia: Diagnosis and Treatment*, there were four hundred and ninety-seven thousand.

Within six months, I had to make the most painful decision of my life. I just could not cope with the crowds. They were even camping on the lawn. Reporters and photographers everywhere. The Council whingeing about double-parking; the Tidy Town Committee about litter on the streets.

I lay awake at night; paced from room to room; drove to Tonelemona and traipsed the bog for miles. And finally I decided. In memory of Mary Margaret and my mother; of the millions who suffered in childbirth, at the hands of husbands, lovers, faces in the dark; in memory of those who suffered at the hands of patriarchial medicine, The Rule of Love would be reserved for women.

I could never have forseen the reaction. The Men's Confraternity, the Chamber of Commerce, the Knights of Columbanus, filled *The Midland Star* with outrage. They scourged me with poison pens; made the women run the gauntlet of their jeers. I was even summoned to the Papal Nunciature. Can you credit that? I refused, of course, and, a fortnight later, this fat black car drew up outside the gates. A chauffeur ran to open the door, and a small black beetle of a man emerged.

As he introduced himself, a wave of olive oil nearly knocked me over. For half an hour, he stood with his back to the window, lecturing me on miracles, Canon Law and

Scripture. He joined his hands and spoke of Padre Pio and the lovely smell of roses, the hem of Saint Martin's cloak, a nun in Barcelona. How the precious gift of healing must be shared equally among all God's Catholic children.

I never opened my mouth, but listened with bored politeness. When he left a space for me to be impressed by some statue that moved in Guatemala, I showed him the door. He scuttled past me, mumbling *'ab homino iniquo et doloso erue me'*. I offered a translation and his shiny shoulders twitched in anger. Then I opened every window in the house.

What is your most treasured possession? See, you have to think. That's how precious it is. Without any hesitation, I can tell you mine. But I'll let you guess. Go on, try. . . .

No. They mean nothing. Nothing at all. What shall it profit a man if he gains the whole world and loses The Alchemy of Love?

These are my most sacred possessions: the memory of Mary Margaret and my parents, The Rule of Love, and a piece of glass. Yes, that's right. A small piece of glass.

Sometimes, when sleep refuses all my prayers; when Cesare's accusations make me weep, I press it against the softness of my cheek. Sometimes I rub my fingers along its edge.

Here's a story for you:

In 1867, my grand-aunt Julia fell helplessly in love with Martin Lalor. She was seventeen, as innocent and beautiful as sunlight. He was Casanova, twice her age, notorious for his ruby ring that dazzled every woman in the county. When her father discovered that his beloved daughter was pregnant, he packed her off to his sister in America. 'Sure aren't they asking her for years?' he reasoned with his wife's tears.

On the night before she was escorted to Queenstown, Julia heard a noise outside her window. Stifling the tears that had not stopped all day, she opened the curtains. The sky was black as pitch; not a breeze disturbed the stillness of the bog. Frightened by the pounding of her heart, she dismissed the sound as the pecking of a bird, the scratching of moths against the window-pane. She lay down again and, trembling at how her parents could still insist they loved her, cried herself to sleep.

Her father pushed her aboard the *Nimrod* and sixty-three days later she landed in New York. She tore up the placard he had scrawled for the aunt who had never seen her, and disappeared through the gates of Ellis Island. Word eventually got home that Julia and the infant in her arms had been crushed to death by a startled horse in Brooklyn.

In 1869, The Big Wind devastated Tonelemona. The roof was torn off every cottage in the village; trees swirled like matches; dogs, cats, even donkeys were carried off across the bog. An ancestor of The Widow Tynan's, demanding fresh eggs for his breakfast, found himself and the henhouse swept away like Dorothy from Kansas.

Poking through the debris, my father's grandfather came upon my miraculous piece of glass. Tears burned his eyes as he read the copperplate inscription — MY DARLING JULIA PURTOCK — made by the ruby ring of Martin Lalor.

Sometimes I trace her name in the darkness and feel humbled by The Alchemy of Love. Sometimes, too, I run the jagged edge along my throat and think how easy it would be.

Anorgasmia. Oopheritis. Dysmenorrhoea. Thrombosis. Ectopic pregnancy. My hands cured them all. I healed schoolgirls frightened by periods and exams; their mothers by the change of life. A farmer's wife who assisted at lambing and lived in dread of losing her first child. A teenager worn out by babies. A spinster addicted to pornography. A famous singer cursed with warts. Little girls who cried in the dark. Old women haunted by the grave.

My only relaxation was to walk the bog at night-time.
What?
Don't be stupid. I knew every sod of turf, every leaf that rustled in the breeze.
In the beginning, I used to call to my uncle's but, after a few minutes' small talk, I knew it was time to leave. Even The Widow Tynan had changed. Sometimes I sat among the cobwebs in my parents' kitchen, but, even there, I felt like an intruder. In the eyes of Tonelemona, I was still an outcast; the traitor who had left them for the town.
And so the bog became my only comfort; my sanctuary; my haven; my escape from the multitudes; my forty days in the desert.

Listen to this. I found it in the dayroom.

The town is noted for the sincere warmth of its welcome and, within a convenient distance, visitors will be charmed by a host of delightful attractions. Chief of these, and the veritable jewel in the natural crown of the area, is the renowned midland bog. Extending in all directions as far as the eye can see, the bogland is a wonder to behold — a vast expanse of unrestrained beauty, with unique flora and fauna, where the traditional way of life is still preserved.

What do you think of that? The sincere warmth of its welcome. Delightful attractions. Am I a delightful attraction? One of their unique fauna? Dragged through the streets. Locked in a cage, spat at by children.

Mary Fenlon couldn't cry. Dead babies, her own wedding day, the lump in her sister's breast, could not provoke a single tear. The reason was simple. She was born without lachrymal glands and so, for thirty years, her life was a nightmare of hourly drops, doctors peddling miracles, hospitals that sent her home, each time more despairing than the last. For thirty years, she was toyed with by Hippocratic fools.

One surgeon with a string of letters longer than his name, swore he had made a breakthrough. He diverted moisture from her salivary glands and, for six months, until she begged him to take the knife to her again, the only time Mary found water in her eyes was when she saw a tasty meal.

Of course I'm serious. Didn't I tell you every word is the

gospel truth.

She was no sooner in the door than she pulled me towards her, promising the earth if I could only make her cry. I eased my hand from hers and she knelt before me like a martyr in a child's prayerbook. When a tiny tear gathered in the corner of each eye, I stood shivering before her, humbled yet again by the generosity of love.

Closer and closer, along the murmuring avenue, until their wings are trumpets in my ear, come the legions of deceit.

Belial Larkin, breathing promises and death.

Chemos Larkin, whose foreign tongue sucked innocence from a child.

Thammuz Larkin, leprous with debauchery.

Dagon Larkin, incubus of water.

Baalim Larkin, whose claws juggled perversity and love.

Moloch Larkin, besmeared with blood and parents' tears.

According to Aristotle, thirty-seven is the ideal age for a man to marry. The perfect age for his bride is seventeen because they would then experience sexual decline at the same time — he at seventy, she at fifty. In their thirty-seventh year, Paul Gauguin left his wife and children; Alfred Adler invented the term 'inferiority complex', and Louis Bleriot made the first ocean-crossing in an aeroplane. Robert Burns, Van Gogh and Marie Antoinette all died at thirty-seven, and I was driven from The House of Love.

ONE MORE NIGHT!

The grounds are crowded; every blade of grass trampled by their prayers. They are even blocking the road outside. The torches remind me of the moneen, and tears sting my eyes. Tears of joy because I know it's only hours before I'll be home with her again. Safe within The House of Love, the tang of creosote burning on our lips.

Someone shouts 'Here's your hearty breakfast', and something bangs against the window. The fools. The poor deluded fools.

Only a few minutes ago, I said goodbye to Cesare and Lucrezia. He shook my hand and I could have sworn he was going to cry. When I asked Lucrezia if she wanted me to heal her bonsai, she got so embarrassed I was sorry I said anything.

Picture them coming for me at dawn, their footsteps getting louder on the corridor. Picture the sleepy faces peeping from a dozen doors. Can you hear the old man singing; see the yellow fingers clawing at his chest?

> I'll fly away. Oh glory, I'll fly away,
> By and by alleluia when I die,
> I'll fly away.

They will roll back the stone, peer into the darkness and find my spirit gone.

Never in the memory of Tonelemona has there been such a storm. My beloved bog is convulsed by water, wind and fire. Rivers thunder from the heavens; banks of turf crumble into mud. Lakes appear from nowhere, swallow bolts of lightning, and disappear again. A million creatures drown and fly screaming through the sky. The earth peels back, exposing fields of ancient stones. The stones are flung away like pebbles. Everywhere is chaos and destruction but — look! look! — standing on the moneen, savouring every sting of rain, every dart of light, his face tilted to the stars, his arms saluting the majesty of fire, is The Alchemist of Love.

My clothes howl in rags around me, but there is exhilaration in my bones.

Heather sizzles; sods of turf are shrapnel; the cromlech is swept away and blasted into sand. A togher squelches to the surface, its wooden beams a zip that flashes once and is gone. Eels are whips against the backs of trees; The Devil's Hole a vortex into hell.

And then, as if I had raised my hand and shouted 'Cut!', the mayhem shudders to a halt. There is no anarchy in the sky, no churning in the earth beneath my feet. No sound at all, but the bog gasping to regain its shape. In front of me, a hare watches his reflection in a pool. Somewhere in the distance, a skygoat calls.

I turn to walk back, to face again the thousands shrieking for my hands, when suddenly I see her. My eyes flutter, my body shakes in disbelief, but no, she does not disappear. She is still there, her perfect hand beckoning me across the bog.

The Alchemist of Love has been rewarded. Her love for Miracle Mickey has triumphed over death. The Mad Maneen has not suffered in vain.

Shouting at the sky, I run and take her in my arms. Every step brings bigger tears. My eyes are blind as I stumble

141

towards the lane. As gently as my father bore me through the yard that Easter morning, I carry her sleeping body to the car. A hundred times I kiss her lips, stroke her cheek, run my fingers through her hair.

Think long on this, my undisbelieving friend. Let every word linger in your ears; for this is how she came back to me again.

For two days and nights she lay sleeping in my parents' bed. Never once did I leave her side, or even close my eyes. And, all the while, The Rule of Love was trembling in her hand. The Rule of Love thinketh not evil; rejoiceth not in iniquity, but rejoiceth with the truth.

Picture this:

It is the third morning and suddenly her body starts to move. Her flesh is shimmering with The Alchemy of Love. She is waking. She is going to turn her head and speak. She is going to crush me in her arms and whisper that she has always loved The Alchemist of Love.

But no — look! look! — she is crying. She is weeping tears of creosote. I fall to my knees and lick the creosote from her cheek, but no matter how I try, calling her name, soothing her with kisses, I cannot stanch the tears. There are shouts from the garden. They are shouting my name, but I cannot let them see her like this. No-one will ever see her so distraught. She will be beautiful when we return to Tonelemona. She will wear the whitest dress. Dandelions will be golden in her hair. She will be the Morning Star, Queen of the May, Our Lady of the Boglands. She is weeping for The Rule of Love. I feel it seething in the marrow of my bones, surging through my blood. But I am powerless. Her flesh is oozing tears of creosote. When the door bursts open, I throw myself upon her and The House of Love evaporates in creosote.